PENGUIN BOOKS

LOVE ON THE SECOND READ

Mica De Leon is a Filipino writer of swoony romance comedy novels and SFF novels. She has won the Don Carlos Palanca Awards For Literature in 2019 and 2022 for her essays on romance, feminism, history, fantasy, and the Filipino identity in the aftermath of Martial Law and the 2022 presidential elections in the Philippines. She likes walking on the beach, dogs, cats, swoony and spicy romance novels, lengthy epic SFF novels, and Taylor Swift.

Connect with her on Instagram and Tiktok: @micadeleonwrites

ADVANCE PRAISE FOR *LOVE ON THE SECOND READ*

'Filled with humour, charm, and enemies-to-lovers swoon, *Love On The Second Read* is an absolute winner! A must-read for rom-com fans!'

—Samantha Young, *New York Times* & *USA Today* Bestselling Author

'Set in the world of publishing and chock-full of literary references, *Love on the Second Read* is the perfect romance novel for book lovers. Emma and Kip will steal your heart!'

—Lynn Painter, *New York Times* Bestselling Author

Love On The Second Read is a delightful enemies-to-lovers romantic comedy perfect for book lovers! Emma and Kip sparkle and shine in this wonderfully witty, banter-filled novel about finding your one and only. Mica De Leon pens a swoony romance sure to charm all readers!

—Jenn McKinlay, *New York Times* bestselling Author

'Charming and sweet with enough bite to keep things interesting, in *Love On The Second Read* author Mica De Leon delivers the rom-com feels readers crave. In a word, delightful.'

—Melonie Johnson, *USA Today* Bestselling Author

'Mica de Leon's debut is witty, heartwarming, and bingeworthy. Romance readers are going to fall in love with the strong and sensitive protagonists and enjoy this book immensely.'

—Ivy Ngeow, *The Straits Times* Bestselling Author of *The American Boyfriend*

Love on the
Second Read

MICA DE LEON

PENGUIN BOOKS

An imprint of Penguin Random House

PENGUIN BOOKS

USA | Canada | UK | Ireland | Australia
New Zealand | India | South Africa | China | Southeast Asia

Penguin Books is part of the Penguin Random House group of companies
whose addresses can be found at global.penguinrandomhouse.com

Published by Penguin Random House SEA Pte Ltd
9, Changi South Street 3, Level 08-01,
Singapore 486361

First published in Penguin Books by Penguin Random House SEA 2023

Copyright © **MICA DE LEON** 2023

ISBN   9789815144031

Typeset in Garamond by MAP Systems, Bangalore, India

www.penguin.sg

*For those whose hearts were broken one too many times before
and are desperate for second chances, this book is for you.
Remember that it doesn't matter how many second chances
you get as long as the last one sticks.*

Love On The Second Read Playlist

I Can See You by Taylor Swift
Shade Of Yellow by Griff
You Belong With Me by Taylor Swift
Deja Vu by Olivia Rodrigo
Nonsense by Sabrina Carpenter
Cruel Summer by Taylor Swift
Hits Different by Taylor Swift
Cornelia Street by Taylor Swift
Watermelon Sugar by Harry Styles
Electric Touch by Taylor Swift
Jealous by Nick Jonas
Never Ending Song by Conan Gray
2 Be Loved (Am I Ready) by Lizzo
Living Proof by Camila Cabello
New Rules by Dua Lipa

Contents

Chapter 1

New Year Announcements

Emma escaped into the fantasy romance in her head.

Today, it went like this: She was running away from this life and leaving for another country where a comfy book editor job with a salary three times her current pay was waiting for her. She packed all her worldly possessions in a single suitcase, the classy kind with a pattern of the brand's logo printed on the leather exterior. The kind she could never dream of affording. The kind that would float to the surface of the ocean in case her aeroplane crashed in the middle of the Pacific. She could fit in it, so maybe she should ride in it if it did sink—

She was going on an odd tangent. Again. She often did this when she was stressed—or on the brink of breaking down. She was too exhausted to pay attention to their publisher discussing last year's sales, which she knew would inevitably end with, 'Please, please, please get your books out on schedule or we don't hit our targets.' It was a subtle jab at the editors, at her specifically because she was the one who was late (again) in submitting the files of her books for next month—Valentine's month, which was just three weeks away.

This was the company's first town hall of the year and the first time all the employees had congregated in person after

Christmas break and the pandemic. They'd been doing this online during the lockdown, which Emma preferred because she could simply throw a blazer over her pyjamas and look professional from the waist up. Janey was, of course, overjoyed that they were meeting in person again. ('Because it's great for collaborations and synergy,' Janey said. Whatever that meant.) In these meetings, the publisher discussed data, sales, projects, marketing plans, events, deadlines, and conglomerate activities and announcements. Janey had explained to Emma in her first couple weeks in the company that these were organized so employees could see how their jobs contributed to the company's success as a whole.

Emma was barely out of holiday mode, and the leftover decor from the Christmas party hanging all over the open office space wasn't exactly helping her get back into the grind. And what about the books she was supposed to turn in at the end of the month for March? And the books she should have already started for April and May. There were the other thirty-plus books for the rest of the year. And the yearly lineup of romance manuscripts for next year that she had to submit in June for approval. Oh, and were those proofs on her desk for checking . . .

Her phone screen lit up, and she picked it up to check the notifications. Two messages. One from her best friend, January Flores (but she'd explicitly told everyone to call her Janey. 'Please. January is my grandmother,' she had said), the company's marketing officer, publicist, social media manager, event organizer—and all the other non-bookmaking jobs of the book publishing business. Everyone was doing three people's jobs in publishing lately. They all blamed it on the dip in sales and the increase in expenses and costs in the two years the world had stopped because of the pandemic—and its aftermath. Not that it ever felt significantly different. Emma remembered being just as exhausted then as she was now, the difference being that she didn't have to commute so much and when she did need to pull in late nights, she could do it in the comforts of her studio unit which she shared with her three rescue cats—Wentworth, Knightley, and Darcy—instead of the office with all the lights turned off except at her workspace, the night guard trying to engage her in conversation every few hours, and ghosts and monsters messing with the keyboards and chairs two rows from her table.

Her phone vibrated in her palm again, and she unlocked the screen to see the messages that came in.

'I think Brent will make the big announcement today!!!' Janey said in her text message, followed by a slew of emojis that Emma could only interpret as an emotional roller coaster. Brent was Maya Press's publisher, who was promoted to the position just three years before the pandemic hit. For as long as any of them could remember, he'd been under pressure to keep the company afloat. It was a testament to his skill as a business manager that Maya Press has stayed in business even through the pandemic.

Energetic, optimistic, and enthusiastic, Janey wasn't any different online and in person, as opposed to Emma who kept to herself. Not because she was a snob, she was just constantly reading and editing and rewriting manuscripts even when she was not at her desk. Emma lived and breathed romance. It was her dream job after all, making romance novels for a living. She just hadn't expected it would be this exhausting (or unprofitable).

She looked up at Brent in his white button-down shirt with the sleeves folded up to his elbows, dark pants, and meticulously swept-back black hair peppered with greys at the side, standing in front of the conference room, facing his employees with a stoic albeit compassionate expression on his face that signalled to everybody that he was about to deliver some very distressing news. 'We haven't been hitting our targets for six months . . . Corporate is skittish . . . ' he droned on.

For a second, Emma's vision blurred, and she imagined Brent as the billionaire CEO in the manuscript she'd had to stop editing before coming to this morning's meeting. She shook her head, and the room came into focus again. She saw the backs of her coworkers' heads. The meeting room was big, too big for a team of twenty people, when once upon a time this room would have been filled with so many people that Emma got claustrophobic. She was small and unassuming and out of the way in the meeting room. Everyone would have to literally turn their whole bodies to look at her where she sat, in the very back. There were two people from accounting and the production manager and the Human Resources (HR) manager at the front table. Circulations (three salespeople and seven warehouse people) occupied the row of tables close to the doorway. The art department (two artists) were in the row across from them, and the editors (three people) sat behind everybody, no doubt hiding from deadlines—and Brent whose pacing up front was making everybody nervous. Janey, with her bright platinum long bob standing out amid a sea of raven-black and brown hair, sat up front with accounting, frantically scanning and typing on her phone. Emma sat right behind her nemesis, sci-fi and fantasy editor Kip Alegre, who smelled like shampoo and detergent today along with that familiar spicy, musky scent of books cracked open for the first time.

She turned her attention back to her phone. 'Don't be ridiculous, Janey. They've been threatening to shut us down for four years. They couldn't do it the first time, they sure as heck won't do it now.'

Then she scrolled down, eyes suddenly drawn to a message she'd received and read earlier this morning before the Monday grind began.

She didn't have to open it to know it said, 'Babe, please talk to me. It's been six months.'

Since she'd broken up with Nick six months ago, her ex had been texting her at least once a week asking to meet. She wasn't ready to see him again in person. It was still too raw, too weird.

She tapped, a little too aggressively on the other new message, her eyes glossing over who it came from.

'Hey, Morales. Thornfield Hall called. Mr Rochester wants you back in his attic,' Kip wrote in his text message, and she rolled her eyes at the back of his head and his overgrown dark brown hair, which fell so messily yet suavely. She couldn't remember when they'd started trying to out-nerd each other, but it escalated to an unspoken contest of literary-themed smackdowns.

She thought she was winning. She could tell that her paltry knowledge of Science-Fiction Fantasy (SFF) books and graphic novels stunned him into shutting up, but then sometimes Kip surprised her with obscure romance references that even she had to Google to understand—thereby making her shut up too. They both liked all types of books. It just so happened that they were assigned specific genres, and so one just had more experience and expertise over a genre than the other. No matter who won a round, they somehow always managed to even out the odds. Not that they were counting. Well, Emma was. She always played to win.

'Go back to your Hobbit hole, Alegre,' she texted back, then added, 'What do you want?'

She watched his shoulders tense, and his head dipped down to look at his phone. 'Jokes on you, Morales. I would love to live in a Hobbit hole,' he replied. 'I need the colour proofer for the Summer Komikon graphic novels. Will you be pulling an all-nighter again?'

'You're too tall for a Hobbit hole, Fool of a Took. And not tonight. Still checking InDesign files,' she replied then moved to press the lock button of her phone when a new message from Janey came.

'It's different this time. The pandemic happened, remember? ZERO SALES!!!'

Brent's voice grew a little louder. 'Okay, announcements from Corporate . . . '

Emma's phone vibrated from more messages from Janey. 'This is really it!!!!', 'Brent will make the announcement!', 'The end times!', and 'I hope we're still friends after this!' Followed by ten more separate messages from her best friend.

'There are updates in the accounting system,' Brent said. 'Check your inboxes for the correct process. We have to digitize our documents soon . . . '

'See, Janey,' Emma replied. 'Just regular boring administrative announcements. Nothing to worry about.'

'You don't understand. Corporate PR hasn't been coordinating with me about company-wide events . . . '

'Isn't that a good thing?' Emma replied to Janey. 'You have way too much on your plate already anyway.'

'Next,' Brent continued. 'Don't forget that we have the corporate sports fest at the end of the March—'

A collective groan resounded in the room.

'Everyone—' Brent yelled to the crowd to stifle the complaints. '—is *required* to participate. We need to make a good impression with Corporate. So, either you tell HR which event you want to play in, or we assign you one event. No exceptions.' Brent looked to Tita Beth, the HR lady (who reminded Emma of a fluffy pink cat she'd seen on TV), who simply waved at everyone with a too-congenial smile.

'If that was Brent's big scary Corporate announcement, then you're right to be overdramatic,' Emma messaged Janey.

'Please. It's just sports,' Janey said with a slew of sports-themed emojis. 'I passed my previous jerk-and-clean record last week.' Arm flexing emoji.

'Moving on. Alignment updates. This year, we need a record-breaking bestseller. I don't care if it's romance or sci-fi or some weird TikTok book that no one's thought of yet . . . '

Emma's attention drifted to the message from her ex again. Whenever she even caught a glimpse of her ex's name in her inbox, she felt her stomach twisting into tight knots. She should erase his contact information from her phone, but what would that do? She still knew all his contact details by heart. And social media was still a viable option. She should block him, of course, but she felt bad breaking off all contact with a man who had been a significant part of her life for the last six years. It was her doing that got them to this point. It didn't feel right to punish him when he was already down, but she owed him that much to remind him that this was the best for both of them.

She began typing a reply, 'Nothing's changed, Nick . . . ' but was unsure if she got to hit the reply button when—

'Morales!' Brent called, startling her into dropping her phone a little too loudly on the table, drawing all eyes to her. Including Kip, who turned around in his chair to face her and pushed his square, black-rimmed glasses up his nose to get a better look at her; his black face mask dangling loosely from one ear. She was distracted by the way the sleeves of his dark, no doubt nerd-themed shirt (*The Lord of The Rings* probably. Or maybe *Star Wars*. He was a nut for *Star Wars*), hugged the arm that he'd hooked over the back of his chair.

'Pay attention, Nora Ephron,' he whispered, grinning smugly at her. She glared back.

Brent continued, 'Any news from your authors? Amora Romero?'

She swallowed, then bit her lip, her mouth feeling dry, and she had the sudden urge to run her hands through her black wavy hair, unsure if she'd even bothered to run a comb through her locks before running to the office from her condo. She resisted. Barely.

'No, Sir. Amora's still dealing with crippling writer's block,' she began to say, wanting to leave it at that, but the look on Brent's face and the almost too violent way he clenched his jaw changed her mind. 'I have some for the September book fair that have been causing a stir among the fans, but none from our bigger bestsellers yet. I expect they'll be sending pitches within the next three months before I present my lineup proposal for next year in June.' She bit the inside of her cheek, hoping to stop herself from saying something she'd regret, but the way everyone was looking at her in the very back of the room, hopeful, expectant, guilt-ridden, made her feel like the fate of the world hung in the balance and she was the only one who could set it right. 'We can pick one and supercharge production timelines to make a December release.'

She slapped herself in her mind over and over and over again. There she went again, making promises she really didn't want to keep. Neither was she capable of keeping them if she were being honest with herself.

Kip clucked his tongue and shook his head, looking at her apologetically, pityingly. He understood what she'd done. He had been forced to make promises he couldn't keep, too. She'd promised a production timeline that would make her year a living hell.

Everyone turned to Brent for an answer. He folded his arms across his chest, looking at Emma with unreadable eyes. He merely nodded. 'Keep me updated,' he said, then turned his attention to his golden boy, Kip, managing editor extraordinaire. 'Kip, any news from that new acquisition? The journalist?'

'She's written two manuscripts actually, sci-fi and literary journalism, both pandemic related. I sent both to your email to choose which one to take if we're only taking one, but we should take both if we can. I personally prefer the non-fiction manuscript, though I doubt it's going to break even in a year or two. She hinted that it's being optioned by an international publisher, but she preferred a local publisher first because we'd be hitting her intended target audience directly and immediately. I really have a good feeling about this book.'

Brent's face flashed with a glimmer of hope, but it was gone in a blink. Hope was easy to snuff out when everybody's jobs were on the line, and it was his job to keep everybody employed. He simply nodded and said, 'Let's talk in my office after this.'

Their publisher was an old hand at making books, an old-school traditionalist who sometimes fell into old ways of thinking (i.e., gendered publishing, perpetuating passé stereotypes, etc.). He knew what it was like to produce books before the Adobe Creative Suite. Heck, he'd have been checking contact prints and proofs on the lightbox in his day. To his credit, Brent was always willing to learn and listen and take big risks where nobody would—if his people gave the right argument. To his discredit, when in doubt, his choices usually went to where the money followed—especially these past four years since rumors of the company folding had first floated around.

Her phone pinged again just as Brent harassed the new junior editor, Jesse, for her book targets.

'The Jane Eyre third act isn't a good colour on you, Morales,' Kip texted. 'The time for self-sacrifice died with Ironman in the pre-pandemic era.'

'Running out of literary references? Admit defeat, Alegre', she replied, then notifications for new messages flashed above the screen—several of them, which could only mean Janey.

Suddenly, Brent stopped pacing, and it was like a hard punctuation at the end of a grave sentence. Try as he might, he couldn't hide the morose look on his face, and a tense, nerve-racking silence fell in the room . . . Even Janey put down her phone to focus on their publisher.

'We've been given one year to try and prove that the company is still profitable,' Brent said.

As if by a cruel twist of fate, her ex replied—'Let's meet. Please? Just to talk? No promises. No expectations.'—to the text that she had sent by accident when she'd dropped her phone.

'If we can't . . . ' Brent shook his head, unwilling to put into words a reality that hadn't come yet, a promise that could still be broken if they just kept fighting. 'You'll all of course be properly compensated, and the company will do all we can to help you transition, but . . . '

Emma didn't hear the rest of it, or rather the rest of the world was drowned out by the thoughts racing to the surface in her head. It was finally happening. Her greatest fear. She was losing her dream job and going back to corporate. What if no one hired her? She literally knew nothing else other than making books. She still had twenty years on her mortgage, debt from her mother's medical bills, three fat, spoiled cats to feed. She'd never make books again. Tears stung the corners of her eyes, and she knew she wasn't the only one in the room whose heart was broken by this piece of news.

She caught herself spiralling and went to the place she went to when the world felt all wrong and particularly hateful: Her romance fantasy. It was how she'd coped with her mother's condition during the pandemic. It was how she'd coped with her relationship with Nick. It was how she coped with the stresses of life.

So she was at the airport, going to that cushy new book editor's job with the six-digit pay cheque. She had one fancy suitcase. She was wearing that fancy dress she had been saving for a special occasion. She had a one-way ticket to a brighter future. And then the love of her life was running after her, with roses and a long-winded speech about why she shouldn't leave because their love was worth the sacrifice. She answered yes without thinking, and they got married, and they lived happily ever after. The end.

She frowned, the claws of reality pulling her back to earth. *Sacrifice? You're going to be very broke soon,* she told herself in her head. *And no way three cats and your hoard of books are going to fit in one suitcase. And who are you kidding? You're more likely to jump in front of a plane taking flight than get back together with your ex.*

This was how her mind worked under pressure. In the last two years of the pandemic—the worst years of her life, she had developed a way to cope with every terrible thing she could encounter. She'd learnt to compartmentalize, created self-contained shelves for specific sections of her life, like a library of bad memories. She'd learnt not to let one spill into another section so that the stress and pain didn't pile up in one go, because one person could only take one bad thing at a time before falling apart. And if she fell apart, she was afraid that everything else would.

Her phone vibrated in her hand. She peered at it through tears and saw an email notification from a name that made her heart race. The romance gods sure had great timing.

'I experimented with this one to get me out of my rut. I think I did all right, but I'm desperate to know what you think', Amora said in her email with an attachment, a finished manuscript entitled, *The Menagerie of Lost Things*.

The message made her laugh out loud, earning her dirty looks from everyone in the room, including Alegre who made the effort to turn around to look at her like he was reading a signpost in another language.

She ignored him and opened the file, feeling a discordant mix of confusion and joy and denied relief swirling in her already addled, exhausted mind.

A text notification from Kip flashed at the top of the screen.

'Never. (Graphic novels *are* literature!) Besides, I've got more up my sleeve, Morales. I'll sweep you off your feet', he replied. It sounded oddly like a promise.

Chapter 2

The Menagerie of Lost Things

The romance author's manuscript was essentially science fiction. Hardcore science fiction. *The Foundation, The Expanse,* and *Wall-E* combined.

Emma mulled over the story she had been reading, again and again, these past two days. The ending made her cry every time, not because it was bad or trashy, but because it was a tragic happy ending, which really didn't make sense when she heard it in her head, but really was the best way to describe the story.

The story was about two genetically modified humans— they were barely human, their bodies being more metal and robot parts than flesh during the timeline of the story.

The female robot, named MAIA (or Memory Analytics Index Accumulator), had been sent by the descendants of the people who fled Earth a thousand years ago to retrieve backup data lost on space expeditions on the planet from machines called D:ECEMBE-R (or Drive: Earth Class Emergency Bilge Extractor and Repository). Only one D:ECEMBE-R, in the worst state of disrepair, remained serviceable, but she had to go back and forth daily to download data from the device to give it time to fully charge its batteries between download sessions. MAIA got a glimpse of what life was like on Earth before the great exodus. It was found that D:ECEMBE-R still collected data after the great exodus. She also got glimpses of D:ECEMBE-R's life as a full human. He was a prisoner given the choice between execution and public service as a biological memory storage. In Act Three, she snuck him back into the space station city, Paraiso, for repair thereby breaking the law of not bringing in detritus from outside the safety shield. They got caught, and she never saw him again. Until . . .

Emma was already tearing up a little just thinking about the ending.

If anything, it certainly proved her point that genre was just an arbitrary line set to categorize books and make selling them easier. It was the perfect marriage between Emma's and Kip's genres of expertise. She knew the romance parts well, but she suspected that there were science fiction elements that aimed to deliver symbols and metaphors that just went over her head.

She considered going to Kip for help, but her pride just wouldn't let her. It felt too much like defeat, and Emma hated losing.

She looked over at Kip who was pacing inside the conference room, visible behind glass walls and doors, his voice muffled as he spoke at the laptop. He must have been yelling if sounds were escaping through the walls. Emma caught sparse phrases from the meeting ' . . . misogynistic men . . . ', ' . . . overly sexualized female characters . . . ', ' . . . fan-service extraneous scenes that do nothing for the story . . . '

She recognized the face of the author who had been perennially late in submitting manuscripts. The author cringed and flinched every time Kip spoke with wide, almost threatening gestures.

Nope. She couldn't give Amora to Kip. She had just gotten out of her rut and written the best manuscript Emma had read in a long time.

She remembered a time from three years ago when she had been especially persistent about deadlines with Amora. Amora had sent in incoherent bits and pieces of a manuscript a week after her deadline, and Emma had called to check on her. She'd just broken down, saying that she had just broken up with her boyfriend. Emma thought she wasn't going to make her targets that year, but Amora somehow bounced back from that and sent in three romance novellas, which, though shorter than her usual fare, were good enough to tide them over the next three years of the pandemic during which the company had to stop producing books and sell whatever inventory they had left.

This new manuscript had taken Amora three years to write, but it was worth the wait.

Maybe it'd help if Emma knew where Amora's mind was at when she was writing this. They hadn't talked in a long time, not since her last book reprints.

Emma took out her phone and dialled her number.

'Emma, I've been waiting for you to call! Have you read it? What did you think?'

'It's so good, Amora! How long have you been thinking about this story? Why did you write this?'

'I'm glad. I wasn't sure it would work, but my husband said that maybe I needed to get out of my comfort zone—'

'Wait! Wait! Wait! Husband? When did that happen?'

Amora laughed on the other line. 'A couple of years into the pandemic. I'm sorry I didn't invite you. We got married at city hall. It was just us and our parents . . . '

'No! Don't apologize. It was the pandemic. Who is he? How did you two meet?'

Emma maintained a mostly professional relationship with her authors, but sometimes, the boundary between their work and personal lives blurred, and they couldn't help talking about what they've been doing outside of making books. Amora was a local celebrity so much so that she was hounded by her fans at her day job as a copywriter whenever they recognized her. This was why she kept her personal life very private, especially on social media.

'He was my friend from high school. He moved back next door to wait out the pandemic, and it just happened. Last year, we thought life's too short to wait, so we got married.' Emma heard Amora move her phone. 'Enough about me. What about you? It feels like forever since we last talked. You and Nick inspired one of my previous novellas, you know? *Love And Other Notes.*'

Emma resisted the urge to cringe. She remembered that story. At the time, she had already suspected that the romance novella about a book nerd and rockstar could have been inspired by Emma and Nick, but this was the first time Amora had confirmed it. 'We broke up.'

'No!' Amora screamed at the phone, and suddenly there was a request for a video call. 'You have to tell me what happened!'

Emma looked left and right. There were the two artists and Jesse at the table spaces, too close to hers to talk. Kip was still in the meeting room, and Brent was locked up in his office working on his tablet. She snuck to the back of the room, past the meeting room and towards the quiet corner of the proofing machine. There, she answered the video call.

Before Amora could ask questions, Emma cut her off by saying, 'It wasn't anything dramatic. We just drifted apart during the pandemic. That's all.'

'But, how? Why? The man was head over heels in love with you! He wrote songs about you!' Amora practically screamed at the phone so Emma had to lower the volume.

Emma pressed her lips in a thin line and sheepishly looked away from Amora's piercing gaze on the screen. 'When I couldn't even confide in him about what happened to my mother, I knew that our relationship wasn't the same way it was before the pandemic.'

Amora gasped on screen, covering her wide-open mouth. 'I mean, even I knew what happened to your mother!'

'I told him we could still be friends, but we should get used to being apart first just so it's not weird between us.'

'But what changed?'

'We just grew apart. That's all. And the lockdowns just made it worse. We don't even fight when we're upset with each other.'

Amora exhaled a big breath. 'This breaks my heart. You and Nick have always been "couple goals" for me. If you didn't get your happily-ever-after, then what about the rest of us?'

'Amora!' Emma said, forcing out a laugh. 'You're practically still a newly-wed. You got your happily-ever-after!'

Amora laughed, too, more genuinely than Emma had. 'You're right, but still! It makes me rethink some of my love stories.'

'Speaking of your stories, *The Menagerie of Lost Things*. It's so different from your usual! It's so good!'

'Thanks! I appreciate that coming from you, Emma. But really, it's all thanks to my husband. He suggested that maybe to get me out of my rut, I had to try other things. So, we agreed to read and watch each other's favourite books and shows. He liked science fiction and fantasy. I liked romance.'

Amora was a compulsive writer. She didn't make outlines or plan her stories before she wrote them. She just had the instinct for story that many old and new writers would kill to get.

'Anyway, I loved *Barbarella*, and I thought what if I spun that story with *Wall-E*. The romance came out naturally.'

Menagerie was nothing like *Barbarella*, but now that she mentioned it, Emma recognized the resemblance. 'I don't have experience with science fiction though, Amora.'

'I know, but you know my stories so I figured there's no person I could trust to do this more than you.'

The meeting room door slammed open, and out came Kip, red in the face and fuming. He was startled when he saw Emma standing there close to the proofer. He hesitated as if deciding whether he should approach her or walk away now that they were looking eye to eye. Emma saved him the trouble and pointed at her phone to indicate that she was on a video call. He nodded and walked away.

Emma turned her attention back to Amora.

'Who was that?' Amora asked.

'Our managing editor.'

'I remember him. Scary . . . ' Then as if realization hit her all at once, her face paled on screen. 'He does all your science fiction and fantasy books, right?'

Emma smirked though it came out awkward on screen, so she just nodded.

'Please, please, please don't make me work with him. I'm barely out of my rut.'

Emma opened her mouth to say that she hadn't thought about it, but that would have been a lie. She *had* thought about it, but only her pride had stopped her from doing it.

If she had been a better editor, she would have already passed the manuscript to Kip. Amora deserved an editor who knew how to help her with what was probably the best story of her career. When Brent found out about this story (inevitable given that she had to send out the memo for this story soon to get budgets and production timelines), he would likely make her give the manuscript to Kip anyway.

'I'll see what I can do, Amora.' Another promise she wasn't sure she could keep. She should really kick the habit.

It seemed to pacify Amora, but it didn't do anything to quell Emma's worries.

Chapter 3

The Publisher

Genre fiction was fiction decked out with the odd bells and whistles that make up a specific genre. Spaghetti westerns had saloons and horses and gunslingers. Romances had meet-cutes and guaranteed happy endings. Science fiction had exotic science or science-y magic. Fantasy had elves, orcs, and magic.

The Menagerie of Lost Things hit all the beats of a romance fantasy, and yet Emma had to admit that there were just some things she wouldn't know what to do with. Not to mention the inconsistencies she couldn't catch because she was unaware of them.

But what would Amora do if there was nothing that Emma could do?

So, Emma took matters into her own hands and went to Brent just before she sent out the memo.

She had been working for this company for six years. She had experience. She has acquired and worked with many of the company's bestselling authors. She had signed Amora Romero.

And, she had trumped Kip many times in literary smackdowns.

(Which he just cancelled out after so that they were back to where they started).

As she took the long walk from her table space to the publisher's corner office on the other side of the floor, she formulated the arguments in her head, and concocted a scenario in which she wasn't forced to pass Amora to Kip without putting up a fight.

One, she had signed Amora in her first year here and had maintained a good author-editor relationship with her over the years. Two, she knew Amora's storytelling and writing process better than anyone. Three, it had taken a long time to convince Amora that she was a good writer and storyteller and to develop a book-production process that catered to her needs. Four, she had taken seminars on caring for mental health in order to learn how to help Amora whenever she was in one of her moods. (Not that she didn't need therapy herself. The pandemic and the subsequent presidential elections were rough on everyone.)

Kip was merciless with his own authors. He maintained a tyrannical, distant, and unmovable relationship with his authors—nothing like the way Emma worked with hers. He was going to break down Amora and then return her to Emma, broken, insecure, defeated, and unable to string two words together to write a story.

Of course, she wouldn't say out loud the arguments she'd already come up with within hearing distance of Kip. One, he'd know immediately that she was plagiarizing Neil Gaiman's essay on genre fiction. Two, it would be a low-key jab at him and the way he treated his own authors—their rivalry hasn't reached that petty low point yet. And three, it'd be like admitting to his face that he was the better editor, which . . . annoying.

It was apples and oranges. She was good at this, and he was good at that. If their rivalry proved anything, it was that they both didn't discriminate between books. She simply had preferences that had nothing to do with her job or the quality of books she read and edited. Same with him.

But she lost her nerve when she saw Kip in Brent's office. So, she lurked in his doorway, barely visible to the two men inside and debated in her head if she should barge in there, hoping that they'd drop whatever they were doing when she announced, 'Amora just passed the greatest manuscript of her career!' Maybe she should just wait. The way they were talking, it looked like a subject so serious she shouldn't even be listening in. Which also made it irresistible for her to listen in.

'You don't have to do it if you don't want to, Kip,' she overheard Brent saying. 'We would understand.'

Kip didn't answer for a long time, and for a moment, she thought Kip was going to storm out. 'I said I'll do it, Brent. Don't worry about it. Worry about the company's future instead.'

'I always worry about that, Kip,' Brent said airily, like he'd just exhaled deeply. 'With life generally returning to normal, we can sell books like we did in the pre-pandemic days again, but Corporate isn't as easy to persuade. To survive this year, we need sure-sells.'

'There are no sure-sells in publishing, Brent. You know that better than I do, but I think we should take this as an opportunity to experiment. Corporate already expects us to fail, so what else do we have to lose?'

'It's out of character for you to be so reckless,' Brent said.

Kip shrugged. 'What else do *I* have to lose?'

Sometimes Emma forgot that Brent and Kip were childhood best friends, considering that Brent was his boss. It was probably partly why Kip was Brent's favourite editor and confided in him more than in anyone else in the office. They had history. They were real friends outside of work.

But they didn't even look like they were the same age. Brent was well-dressed and carried himself with the air of a man who had the world in the palm of his hand. Kip was much more laidback and relaxed, like nothing in the world could bother him as long as they left him alone with his books and stories and nerd-dom. In fact, Kip almost looked as young as Emma even though he was older than her by five years.

'I say, if we're going out, we might as well go out with a bang,' she last heard Kip say before Brent noticed her standing there.

'Emma, what are you doing lurking outside my office?' Brent called, putting down his clasped hands. 'Come in here.'

Kip looked over his shoulders, his back straightening as she passed him. He opened his mouth to say something—probably some clever quip but changed his mind when he remembered where they were. They had an unspoken rule to keep their little rivalry low-key. Instead, he sat down on the sofa pushed up against the wall, apparently not done with his barrage for Brent.

She took the spot Kip had left and switched glances between the two men in the office, one looking at her back, and the other in front of her, looking like an intimidating boss evaluating a new employee. She considered asking for privacy, but then that felt too much like admitting defeat. And what were the chances that Brent confided in Kip after she left his office?

'What is it, Emma?' Brent asked, pulling her out of her thoughts. He was rolling his wedding band, a thick white gold vine-style ring with a single diamond embedded in the metal, around his ring finger.

'Amora Romero sent a manuscript today, Sir,' she said, trying to remember her argument, but her mind had become a jumble of odd thoughts, of Neil Gaiman, of spaghetti westerns, of Amora's mental health issues.

'That's good, right?' Brent added. 'Is something wrong with it? Is it bad?'

'No, Sir. Actually, it's the best story of her career,' she said. 'We'd be idiots to pass on this manuscript.'

'So, what's the problem?' Brent asked, impatient.

'It's science fiction romance, Sir,' Emma said.

'So, give it to Alegre,' Brent said.

'No!' Emma practically yelled without thinking, all the arguments and opening statements she had planned to make thrown out the window just like that. She facepalmed herself in her mind.

She felt Kip's eyes boring into the back of her neck. If there was anything she hated, it was admitting defeat, admitting an inability to accomplish a task because she was insufficient, not enough. So, she just came out with it.

'I don't trust Alegre with Amora. He'll break her down after I've worked so hard for her to trust me.' She didn't realize that she was talking so fast till she drew in a deep breath at the end.

This was when Kip spoke up, 'You know I'm not mean to my authors on purpose, right? It's nothing personal. I'm just doing my job.'

She flashed him a momentary look, expecting antagonistic energy to be projected at her. Instead, she saw disappointment and guilt, like he was surprised that she'd seen him this way all along. Then she faced Brent who had leaned back into his chair.

'Sir, you wanted a manuscript from a best-selling author, and we got one—from the author who makes us the most revenue no less. All I ask is that you don't take Amora from me. She trusts me. She doesn't know Alegre.' And as if she was driving in the final nail to the coffin, she added, 'Amora asked that she work with me on this.'

Brent didn't move from his seat, but he eyed her with his piercing brown eyes like he was studying an insect pinned on a tray. 'Kip has more experience with science fiction, Emma.'

'I have experience with Amora.'

'Can you promise to have this book out before the Christmas rush?'

Emma's jaw dropped. She had planned to study the genre while editing the manuscript, which meant that she needed more time with it than with her regulars. Plus, she had already promised to produce other books faster than the standard work schedule would permit.

Brent knew the answer before he even asked. Emma wouldn't be able to deliver this book within a timeline that would make its revenue count for Corporate.

'Emma, you know what to do,' Brent said, nodding unapologetically yet gently like he was laying down a dying bird in its nest. He leaned forward to his desk and picked up his iPad to read a manuscript that was already open there. 'Copy-furnish me when you email Kip. I want to see this book, too.'

'But what about what Amora wants?'

'If she trusts you, she can learn to trust who you trust,' Brent said without looking up from his iPad, effectively dismissing them both.

She turned around sharply to look Kip in the eye. He was already standing and waiting. For what, she didn't know. He hadn't said a word as this happened, and it annoyed her that he was taking this so lightly.

She stormed out without saying another word.

Chapter 4

The Art of the Breakup

It felt too much like a breakup, drafting that email to Amora.

In most romance novels, there was always the inevitable breakup scene where the main character and the love interest were separated either by force or by choice, and they tried to settle into a life that didn't have the other in it. The prospect was always bleak. It was the romance equivalent of SFF's *dark night of the soul* trope in the standard hero's journey.

The words she had written in the email felt like a bunch of disjointed platitudes stuck together, which really was how breakups were done anyway. An exchange of empty phrases to make the other feel better about this major life decision, but that still sure as heck hurt to hear. 'It's not you, it's me.' 'The last six years have been fun.' 'I'm not the right fit for you at this time.' 'I'm sure you'll find someone much more worthy of you.'

Once she'd pressed send, she no longer had the motivation to work for the rest of the day so she packed up her things to go back home. Deadlines notwithstanding.

On the way to the door, she passed Kip, who did a double take and then ran after her.

'Hey, Anne Elliott,' Kip said, suddenly walking side by side with her in the hallway. He towered over her in a dark blue

Cosmere shirt, the kind he had to ship from abroad for a courier rate double that of the merchandise's actual price. *Nerd.*

'I already sent the email, Alegre,' she answered without stopping or even looking at him.

He stopped momentarily as if stunned that she hadn't engaged him, then scurried after her to open the glass door for her. But their hands reached for the handle at the same time, one pushing, the other pulling at it, thereby keeping the door closed.

Emma glared at Kip, startling him. He was so jumpy in person, so very different from the man she had watched get into a yelling match with an author earlier that day. 'What do you want?'

'I get the impression that you're mad at me, Emma,' Kip answered, hand still on the door handle.

'Me?' she grinned, her cheeks puffing up from the effort. 'I'm not upset. Why would I be upset? I just gave you my most flight-risk author, the one who has worked with me on nine books. Why would I be upset?' The last words came out as a growl.

Kip stared at her, searching her face for clues, his own face a puzzle of confused thoughts and feelings. 'What if I declined the project?'

'I already sent the email, Kip.' Emma shook the door handle to force it open, but Kip held it steady. His arm, toned and surprisingly big under that loose-fitting nerd shirt, flexed in the process.

'You can still recall it. It hasn't been an hour since you sent it.'

'Brent has probably read it. You've read it already for god's sake.'

'I'll deal with Brent.'

She shook the door handle again, more desperately this time, feeling like she was about to cry. She didn't want Kip to see her cry.

'You won, Kip! Walk away!' She shook the door again, harder, more persistent now, but Kip wouldn't let go.

'What are you talking about?'

Emma saw from over his broad shoulders that they were attracting attention from their coworkers. She sighed. 'Look. You're the better editor. No one but you can do Amora's new manuscript justice. You happy? You won.'

'But Amora trusts *you*. I'm not sure she'd open up to a new editor so easily. Especially someone who scares her.'

Emma's brows wrinkled, and she narrowed her eyes at him. Had he heard her conversation with Amora? She let go of the door handle.

'Brent was right. If Amora trusts me, then she will learn to trust who I trust.'

'Do you really trust me, Emma?'

She shrugged. 'It's not like I have a choice, do I?'

His hands fell off the door handle, allowing her to leave, but he followed her out into the elevator lobby. She jabbed at the elevator button, but the numbers over the doors were a bajillion floors away from her. *Come on! Come on! Come on! Hurry up!*

'Wait, Emma.'

She let out a big breath, her shoulders slumping before turning to face him with an expression that said, 'This better be good.'

'I don't feel good about this.'

'What do you want me to say, Kip?' she hissed at him under her breath. 'That I'm happy I'm giving my best author, the one I have worked so hard on to trust me unconditionally with her stories, to an editor who I know would break her? All because

I wasn't good enough for her. You win, Kip. I get it. You're the better editor. Will you just please leave me alone?'

Kip hesitated, as if at a crossroads of indecision again, like this morning when he'd seen her at the proofing machine on the phone. He looked like he was either about to close the distance between them or flee from her like a rabbit catching sight of a feral fox.

She averted her face from him, embarrassed by her outburst.

Of course, her phone ringing was the perfect excuse to break away from this awkward turn of events, and she fumbled for it in her bag until she found it and answered the call without looking at who it was.

'Hello, babe—Sorry, Ems. I'm not used to it yet. I'm so glad you finally answered.'

'Nick, now's not a good time.'

'I was just wondering if you would like to go to dinner with me this weekend. Just as friends. You said we can be friends, right?'

'Nick, it's still awkward between us.'

'No . . . No . . . I get it. It's just—'

'I'll think about it, okay?' The numbers on the elevator dinged on the floor just above her office's. 'I need to go, Nick.' She dropped the call without waiting for him to answer. When she looked up, she jumped back when she saw Kip still standing there.

'Your boyfriend?' he blurted out, his throat bobbing up and down from a hard swallow.

'My ex,' Emma said. 'Look . . . Sorry, for uhm . . . blowing up on you like that. I just . . . Please take care of Amora.'

'No . . . I . . . uhm . . . I understand why you're upset,' he said, a slender hand, calloused from a career of writing and holding pens, pressing on the back of his neck, but neither of them had walked away. 'I'm here, you know, to help . . . with the manuscript, I mean, not with your boyfriend—but if you do need help there, too.' He closed his eyes and pressed his lips into a thin line like he'd realized his blunder and walked away, back through the office doors, without saying another word.

That was . . . awkward . . .

'Thanks,' Emma said to an empty lobby, just as the elevator door opened for her.

Chapter 5

Antagonists and Villains

The perfect antagonist was oftentimes the one with goals diametrically opposed to the protagonist's. They were not necessarily bad people, but they kept the main character from getting to their goals.

Villains were things of evil.

Like the stationary bike that she'd been riding hard for the better part of an hour while the coach yelled platitudes and incoherent words of encouragement at them like a drill sergeant. This was Janey's idea of girls' day. SoulCycling on a bright Saturday morning after pulling in a late night for work. Janey had already signed both of them up for hot yoga before lunch.

'Next time, I get to pick what to do for girls' day,' Emma said, between pants, her sweaty hands sliding on the handles of her bike.

Janey didn't even look like she was struggling. 'You said you wanted to see who my new beau was.'

'How could you even think about that while doing this?'

'Easy. Hot teacher!' She flicked her chin forwards to gesture at the coach on the lead bike.

Emma had to stop for a bit, her legs were beginning to chafe. 'He's your boyfriend?'

Janey didn't stop. 'Not yet,' she said with a mischievous glint in her eye, sweat finally beading along her hairline. Not a lot, but enough to make Emma feel okay about stopping to catch her breath.

'You know, if the tables were turned, you'd be considered a sexual predator.'

Janey rolled her eyes. 'Please. The power dynamics among gender identities haven't yet tipped in the non-heteronormative male's favour. I embrace my sexuality, it's me taking sexual power for myself. If a man treats me like I'm an object of sexual desire, my value as a person is being diminished. The other way around happens, and the hetero-man's place in society doesn't budge.'

'How can you talk so much while doing that?'

'I don't see pedalling in the back, ladies!' the coach yelled from the front, looking over other bikes at Janey and her.

Emma pedalled again, trying and failing to follow other people's pace. Janey just pedalled a little faster.

'Easy,' Janey said, finally winded, but Emma suspected that it was more from talking so much than exercising. 'I'm trying to make a good impression on the hot coach.'

'Right,' Emma said, just trying to survive the last ten minutes of the class. Why did it feel like she had to pedal for another hour? Things of evil, these stationary bikes were.

***

Three hours later, after an hour each of SoulCycling, hot yoga, and weightlifting, Emma came out of the shower in a towel feeling like her body was made of jelly. The kind that went splat when dropped on the floor.

She sat on the bench in front of her locker as she rummaged through her bag for her phone. She hadn't looked at her phone since this morning. She felt her stomach churn when she saw Amora's name in the notifications along with a couple of other emails.

'I saw your email. Is this story really out of your league?' Amora asked.

Emma didn't know how to reply without looking like a bumbling idiot. She was a decent editor, and she understood the romance parts of the story just fine.

Janey came out of the shower in a bathrobe (because of course she brought a bathrobe to the gym) and a towel wrapped around her platinum hair. 'What is it? You look like you lost a lot of money on cat show bets.'

'I *have* lost a lot of money betting on cats,' Emma said, still frowning at her phone. 'Amora texted me. I promised her I wouldn't give her to Kip if I could help it.'

'Oh god, your flight-risk author will go to Kip? Why? I thought she wrote romance?'

'She did, but her new genre-bending manuscript is romance and hardcore science fiction. Brent made the decision.'

'You could have fought for it. Kip would have yielded to you, no problem.'

'I could have, but I'm adult enough to admit that the best thing for this manuscript is—' She cut off her own sentence, narrowing her eyes in realization, then looked at Janey suspiciously. 'What does that mean? Kip would yield to me no problem?'

'I mean, Kip just looks like he can beat a person up, but he's actually a softie.' Janey smiled conspiratorially at Emma. 'Why? What did you think?'

She hadn't thought about Kip that way. Not the way his arm flexed when he held the door open. Not the way his forehead creased while he read. Certainly not the way his dimples showed on his cheeks even when he was holding back a smile, or the way he always smelled like books.

Her eyes went wide, as she caught herself remembering such specific details about a man she supposedly hated so much right now but couldn't bring herself to actually hate.

'Nope! You're not baiting me again. I've had it enough with men. I've still got Nick to deal with.'

'Nick? Are you getting back together?'

'No! We ended our relationship amicably. I just accidentally answered his call last night, and now he's asking me what my dinner plans are for tonight.'

'And?'

'Aren't we going out tonight?'

'Good answer. Hoes before bros.'

'I believe the phrase is sisters before misters.'

'Not tonight. We be hundred per cent hoes tonight if I can do anything about it. Speaking of . . . ' She grabbed Emma's gym bag out of her hand and rummaged through it. 'What are you wearing? It better be the skimpiest outfit you own.' She frowned and took out beige panties with a cartoon pattern of the black cat from *Coraline*. 'Are you really going to wear this later? What if you decide to get down with a dude, huh?' Emma moved to grab the underwear from Janey's hand, but she extended her arm, keeping the fabric away from Emma's reach. 'It'll be sexier if you went without, but then . . . Maybe they'll find it cute . . . ' She let Emma take it.

'I'm not getting naked with another man.'

'Why? You have a Gandalf situation happening down there?' Janey leaned to look under Emma's towel, which Emma immediately held down.

'What do you mean a "Gandalf" situation?'

'You know . . . ' She mimicked Ian McKellen from the movie scene. *'You shall not pass!'*

Emma scowled, and Janey laughed as she unwrapped the towel from her hair to pat it dry.

Emma was taking the momentary lull, while Janey was busy with her hair, to read the other notifications when Brent called her.

'Kip begged off the *Menagerie* project.'

'Are you giving me back Amora? Why?'

'No. And I told him no. I still want him on the project. He came up with the compromise of you liaising with Amora about the edits you two agree on beforehand.'

Emma was speechless. She had expected Brent to be adamant about this, but Kip, as promised, had 'dealt with Brent'.

'Thank you, Sir,' she replied.

'Don't thank me. Explain to Amora your work setup with Kip. Just make sure this manuscript comes out on time, okay? And set up a meeting with her. I'd like to give initial inputs into the project as well as explain contract issues with this story.'

'Yes, Sir,' Emma said, ending the call and setting down her phone.

'You look like you won the lottery,' Janey asked. 'Who were you talking to?'

'Brent. He gave me back *Menagerie*, on the condition that I worked with Kip on it.'

'Hey, that's a compromise, right? He's not a bad guy after all.'

'Who? Brent or Kip?'

Janey grinned but didn't answer. 'Why am I not surprised that Brent is working on a weekend?'

'Why?'

'His wife gave birth just last month.'

'Well, we might be losing our jobs at the end of the year. I say he better work his ass off trying to keep our jobs.'

'Thanks, Ems. I knew our day needed a dose of pessimism.'

'You know me.'

'But we're still going out tonight, right?'

'Of course. We've got reason to celebrate now.'

Janey went to get dressed in the dressing rooms.

Emma pulled up her chat box with Kip, which was just a long tirade of literary smackdowns, and began typing a message.

'Thanks, Wit,' she started, remembering how his nerd shirt pulled at his big, tight arm when he held the door closed, then followed it up with 'Talk soon about initial edits?'

'Sure, Hoid. I'll be in the office every day all week.'

Chapter 6

Damsel in Distress

Nerds came in different flavours, different iterations, different shapes, forms, names, and personalities. What they all did have in common was the singular passion for what they loved most—and usually it was a thing that was with them when they most needed help.

For Emma, it was books, romances, fantasy, science fiction, contemporary, literary, poetry—everything she could get her hands on. She'd turned to *Nancy Drew*, *Harry Potter*, and *Ender's Game* when she felt alone in school after her dad left their family forever. She'd turned to *Twilight*, *Fifty Shades of Grey*, and *Outlander* when it was difficult with Nick. She'd turned to Jane Austen, the Brontë Sisters, and Emily Henry when she felt so alone during the term of her mother's sickness. She never even got to say goodbye, or hug her, or tell her how much she loved her in person. When they took her away, she never came back. She was just . . . gone.

So, she was a true-blue book nerd.

Of course, her tiny studio unit was mostly bookshelves on every open wall and towers and towers of books scattered all over the floor. Her three cats wove between the towers of books like hamsters in a maze.

She set her laptop on the desk facing the floor-to-ceiling window overlooking the cityscape at night and changed out of her office casual dress and shoes into her most comfortable *pambahay*, an extra-large white shirt that fell to her knees, the front of which was a print of a movie poster, the last *Star Wars* film with Rey and Kylo Ren. It was faded from overuse—so faded that the Chewbacca print was a brown blob over her right boob. Nick had got it from an event he went to—he was a musician, the lead singer of his band—then left it here and forgot about it altogether. He wasn't into nerd stuff like her.

She took out her contacts in the bathroom and pulled on her big, round, metal-rimmed spare glasses. Barefoot, she went to the refrigerator to get food, forgetting that she had forgotten to fill it again. It was a thing her mother had done for her while she was at work. It was one of those things taken for granted until it was gone completely. And suddenly, she was choking up a little and feeling like an idiot for tearing up over an empty fridge. She pulled out the bag of a loaf of white bread she'd been rationing and took out a slice, careful to close the bag again tightly to be returned to the refrigerator. Her cats, Wentworth (grey and black stripes), Knightley (white with splotches of orange), and Darcy (pure black and blue eyes), trailed behind her, slinking around and between her legs, meowing like crazy. Either happy to see her or happy that she was finally home to feed them. She was never sure which, cats being cats. She placed three handfuls of dry cat food into their bowls next to the doorway and kitchen counter. She crouched next to her cats, watching them feast too fast on cat food while she nibbled at her own sad piece of white bread.

Since the company started requiring employees to come to work at least once a week, she had had to drastically change her routine, and her cats resented her for it, for a while.

Or she imagined that her cats felt very strongly about her leaving them alone in the unit more frequently now that the pandemic lockdowns had been lifted. She liked the idea of living things waiting for her when she went home. She figured it must be more drastic for Alegre who lived in Antipolo and who had taken it upon himself to come to the office every day. She couldn't, for the life of her, understand why he did that. The gas alone must be eating up so much of his salary! But then, he was middle management, so probably not a lot.

From her periphery, she caught a glimpse of her phone lighting up on the table next to the laptop, which she opened.

'Enough brooding, Bella Swan. I sent you an email,' Kip messaged her.

'I wasn't brooding, you Hobbit.' But of course she was brooding. She didn't know what possessed her to add more to her reply. Maybe she was lonely. Maybe she was feeling a little out of control. Maybe she didn't want to feel alone. 'And I'm more of a Katniss Everdeen, Ser FitzChivalry.'

'Still a broody MC,' he replied. 'I prefer Hobbit over Fitz. Fitz gets beat up all the time. Bad omen.'

'I meant to say that.'

'Mean. If I get whisked away to a faraway kingdom, I'll help your cats in the uprising when I escape.'

She couldn't help grinning and shaking her head at the Robin Hobb reference as she sat in front of the desk. She did suspect that her cats were plotting against her, and sometimes she thought maybe she should have adopted a dog instead.

She opened his email and the attached Word document with the file name: TMOLT_Initial Thoughts.doc. Brent was copy-furnished in the email.

'All right, Alegre, you mess with my author, you mess with me,' she muttered to herself—and maybe her cats, if they were listening. She tied her hair up into a messy bun on top of her head, unclasped her bra from behind, and took it out through a sleeve before diving into work.

She wasn't as organized as Kip was with her files, and this Word doc was a testament to that.

She liked establishing a sense of order and balance in every aspect of her life. It allowed her to see the variables that she could control and adjust when there was trouble. Kip had a more tyrannical approach to his job. He established the rules, the parameters, and the limits of a project he was assigned at the very beginning and expected everyone to stay in line from ideation to post-production. If they were authors themselves, she'd be a gardener or the pantser, and he'd be an architect or the plotter.

But the thing about Kip that really grated her showed up when he was not playing book editor. When he was off the clock, he had a devil-may-care attitude towards everything in life and avoided altercations as much as possible. During a company team-building trip, Kip had been up against the logistics manager, a burly man who lifted weights during his free time, in a game that would have determined which teams took first and second place and it had all been up to Kip. So, he'd made an excuse to leave and hadn't come back till dinner time.

Kip didn't play unless he knew for sure he'd win. He only ever put up a fight for the things he loved, which were books.

It took her a while to sort through his edits, and two hours had passed by the time she looked up from her laptop, next to which was a yellow pad with her own scribbles and thoughts about Kip's edits.

Her biggest caveat with his edits: He was suggesting a complete overhaul of the story structure to better accommodate the magic system.

'It's forcing itself to hit romance beats that feel adjunct to the storytelling,' said one of Alegre's notes. 'It would serve the story better if she moved certain scenes up and some down. She also wasted the opportunity to build dramatic tension using the rules of the in-world magic system that she herself is trying to establish.'

She began to compose a reply, beginning with 'But the relationship is the point of this story, Alegre—the thing that Amora is best at . . . '

It was midnight when she'd finished and sent back her reply. She didn't know how they were going to tell Amora these edits in a way that would encourage her to revise, not break down and give up altogether.

Working with creatives was like herding cats. Some could be so delicate that they'd scratch you if you so much as flinched around them. Some cats ignored you until they felt like you were worthy of their attention. And then, there were some cats that were so affectionate they would never leave you alone for a single second. Finding that delicate balance and establishing trust with each cat was key to making Emma's job work.

It was why she'd had to argue with management on certain decisions made about some authors. She tried her best to protect her authors' best interests—a job that no doubt a literary agent would be doing if they were based abroad in New York or London, but in the end, she was still employed by the publishing house. She was on their payroll, and she could only do so much to defend her authors without risking losing her job.

She could feel that this thing with Amora would be one of those precarious situations. She was getting rashes just thinking about the stress that would come from this.

This will not stress you out, Emma. You are a professional editor with years of experience. You can deal with this without flipping out.

She closed her eyes and imagined herself at the beach this time, running along the shore, her feet sinking into the wet sand. And there he was, the love of her life, running towards her with open arms and, oddly, a *The Lord of the Rings* shirt.

Her eyes flew open, and she sat back up abruptly in her chair. *What the fuck was that?*

She shook the scenario out of her head, thinking that maybe she should be going to bed by now, but she had been having trouble sleeping these past two years. She'd only be wasting time staring at the ceiling trying to convince her stupid brain to sleep.

So, she opened up the folder of the March books instead. She might as well get some work done.

Which, of course, was the best argument she could tell herself for why she should doomscroll on her phone instead till she fell asleep. And there were messages that she hadn't checked yet. Some were from scammers offering jobs, loans, and credit card debt reminders. There were still the many thousand messages from Janey who was giving her overly detailed descriptions of the guy she'd gone home with the night they went out. Her text chain with Kip, and then right below that were unread messages from Nick.

'Dinner tonight? I'll go to your office.'

'It'll be quick, I swear.

'I was in the building to meet vendors when I thought maybe you could spare a moment for dinner.'

'I remembered you work so late you forget to eat sometimes.'

'I'm in your office's lobby.'

Two new messages came in from Nick.

'Your co-editor told me you left early.'

'Are you home? I'll pick up food on the way.'

'Don't!' she managed to text back. She grabbed her keys, put on the first pair of shoes she could pick up on the way out—worn-out, neon green Quiapo rubber flip-flops she used for laundry day, and ran out of the condo.

She'd made it to the ground floor of her office's building when she saw Nick coming out of the revolving glass door. Of course, he would. Of course, the universe would dictate this perfect timing. She held her breath, her mind blanking out on her. What had she been thinking running out like that? In her ratty pyjamas no less? What did she expect to do? Physically stop him from going to her unit? The condominium building had guards for that! Not to mention that her ex was much bigger and taller than her.

Nick saw her immediately, standing frozen on the spot, and he smiled at her as if nothing had changed between them. A pang shot through her heart at the sight of that easy, familiar way he gravitated towards her—and her to him. Like celestial bodies, planets, moons, asteroids, in a constant push and pull with the sun. He wore a black shirt that hugged his chest snugly, the short sleeves folded closer to the corners of his shoulders, and dark jeans. His hair was slicked back in a way that looked effortless, as if he'd only needed to run his fingers through his hair when he'd woken up that morning. He carried himself as if ready for an attack, thick arms tense, hands balled into fists, face scowling. A warning for any pitiful human who dared look him in the eyes—all except Emma, for whom he softened like butter cut by a hot knife. Nick was the bad boy who fell in love with the good girl, and Emma was the good girl who was supposed to change him for the better. That was until Emma had decided that it wasn't her job and had broken up with him altogether. No explanations. No preamble. No expectations for him to try and change for her. Just a clean cut. Well, not so clean if he was here.

She took one step back when he was just an arm span away from her. He stopped when she flinched.

'Go home, Nick,' she said, so softly that she didn't feel the bite that she'd intended to lace her tone. She couldn't even look him in the eye. 'I'm not ready for this yet.'

He moved to reach for her hand, but she stepped away, clasping her hand behind her.

'Please, Emma. I missed you.'

She bit her lip, swallowing the tears and trying to force the words out of her mouth. It was the gravitational pull again, drawing her to him, telling her to fall back into their old ways. It hadn't been that long since she'd broken up with him. Only six months had passed. It was difficult to forget someone she'd molded her entire life around, so much so that when she left him, there was a hole in her life in the shape of him. Next to the space her mother had left. She couldn't have held on to him when she was broken herself. They were two meteors that once fell together, now tracing different paths across the sky.

'Nick, please I need time . . . ' Tears stung the corners of her eyes. The shelves and compartments in the library of her mind were toppling over. Control slipping through her fingers unsettled her.

'Emma?' said a man who had just slipped out through the revolving doors.

Nick stole a quick glance over his shoulder at Kip but brought his focus back to Emma, grabbing her forearm to pull her closer to him. 'Let's talk in your unit. Please?' he said, desperate, trying to keep the impatience out of his voice.

'I thought you went home,' Kip said, standing next to Emma and switching glances between Nick and then her, who couldn't even look him in the eyes out of shame. 'I need your comments on the file I sent you. Brent wants to see tomorrow morning.'

That reminder of work she'd already done—work that she'd managed to control—was enough to pull her out of her stunned stupor. She pushed Nick's hand off her arm and backed away. 'Go home, Nick. I have . . . work to do.'

Kip positioned himself forward, between Emma and Nick. 'Everything good here, bro?'

Nick's jaw clenched, the softness reserved for her was gone, and in its place was the bad boy she'd once loved. For a second, she thought he'd make a scene, staring Kip down with the aggression of a hungry hound in a cage, and she pleaded him with her eyes that he wouldn't.

'You said we can still be friends, Emma. You promised,' Nick said before storming off.

She covered her face with her hands, willing her tears not to fall, willing herself not to show weakness, a lack of control here at her place of work, here with her co-editor Kip, her mental library falling into disarray. She felt the knots in her stomach coil taut within her, making her nauseated, making her feel guilty, making her feel out of control.

'Emma?' Kip said, making her look up from her hands. His gaze was on her, serious and thoughtful and intense, the valley between his brows deepening, like he was trying to figure out an especially difficult edit on a manuscript. There were no traces of pity. Or guilt. Only . . . concern?

'I'm fine,' she murmured, an effort to deflect the questions that she knew he wanted to ask. 'I sent my comments earlier.' She should walk away. She should go home and hide under her covers before the dam broke and she herself broke down.

'I know. I saw them,' he said, looking left and then right at the street and the people walking along the sloping pathway. 'I'll walk you home.'

'No need. Condo's just that way,' she said, pointing at a pathway that branched to the side. 'I'm not a damsel in distress,' she added, an attempt at flippancy.

'I know,' he said, adjusting his backpack with the rolled-up proofs sticking out of it. 'I just happen to be walking in the same direction as you, Princess Buttercup.' And he led the way to her condo, forcing her to follow without question.

The knots uncoiled. '*The Princess Bride* is barely a romance...'

'Agree to disagree, Buttercup,' he said, pressing his palm on the back of his neck. She had to tilt her chin up to look at his face. He was a big man with such great posture, considering he, like her, spent most of his day hunched over a manuscript. 'It is a love story though so it should count for something.'

'Uh-huh, sure, Inigo Montoya,' she said with a mock roll of her eyes, noticing only now that she'd already forgotten the pang in her chest that was still definitely there.

'Emma, may I ask you a personal question?' he said after a few minutes of guilt-ridden silence from her on the way to her condo's lobby.

She pressed her lips into a thin line, but she nodded, ready to dodge questions about her love life.

'What are you wearing, you big nerd?' he asked, bemused, looking at her with an arched eyebrow.

Well, that was anticlimactic. 'What?' was the only sensible answer she could think of, folding her arms over her chest and remembering that she wasn't wearing a bra underneath this.

He squinted through his glasses at the brown blob print on her shirt. 'Is that Chewbacca?'

'These are my sleeping clothes!' she said, mortified and standing still, voice two decibels higher than she intended. 'I panicked!'

He laughed and flicked his head to point at the glass doors of her condo building. 'This is you, right?'

She turned away from him, arms still folded over her chest. 'Right. This is me,' she said, walking to the doors.

'See you at the office, Katniss,' he said, turning to leave.

She chased after him. 'Kip, wait!'

'What is it, Emma?'

'Thank you . . . ' she said, which elicited a smile that she had never seen on him before.

Huh. Who knew he could smile like that? Unironically. Genuinely.

'Good night, Princess Buttercup,' he said, this time waiting for her to go into the building before leaving.

'Good night, you Hobbit.'

And then as the elevator doors closed, she caught a glimpse of Kip going back where they came from.

Chapter 7

The Deal

Emma wished that life was as cleanly structured as a story.

Promise-progress-payoff. The three act structure. The hero's journey. The romance arc.

Her life would have been so much easier if she could categorize events in her life as necessary beats in a story. Because then she could predict how the story ended. Adopting her cats would definitely be a pet story, like *Hachiko* or *The Art of Racing in the Rain*. But come to think of it, cats, hers specifically, were assholes. Nick would have been a pocketbook story, like the ones adapted from whatever story website was going viral that year, where good girls fall in love with the bad boys who changed for them. Definitely fiction, that one. People didn't change, they only settled into who they were as they grew up and grew old. Her mother's death would be contemporary fiction about a woman rising from the ashes and defying all else for love, for her daughter, for herself.

She did not know whatever beat this meeting was hitting with Brent leaning back into his chair behind his desk and Kip standing, face red and posture tense, in the heat of an argument with her, as she tried and failed to match his angry posture. This was one of the few times she wished she inherited her father's genes instead of her mother's.

She hated being shorter than Kip, but then, Kip was a giant compared to average men. So, Emma was *extra* short compared to Kip.

Turned out, that one night that Kip had walked her home had been a free pass, but who had she been kidding, thinking Kip had changed or at least mellowed for her? Work Kip had always been an asshole compared to After-Hours Kip.

They'd been going back and forth on *Menagerie*, neither side compromising their stance on how to fix this particular manuscript. Of course, it didn't help that Brent sided with Kip almost all the time. Meanwhile, Amora trusted only Emma with her stories.

It was an odd place to be, fighting for her author so she could keep her job and fighting with her boss so Amora didn't terminate her contract and take her stories elsewhere—which, if that happened, would result in Emma losing her job anyway.

Damned if you do. Damned if you don't.

Emma thought this was the inciting incident or at least the event leading up to the scene where Amora took back her manuscript and stopped writing stories altogether.

This meeting was for them to finally sit down with Amora and discuss their edits point by point, and up until this morning, she and Kip had only come up with a page-by-page compilation of the edits they agreed on, all the while remaining adamant on the fifty pages each they'd both prepared for this meeting. These were the major edits on which neither she nor Kip were willing to budge.

The Menagerie of Lost Things was a love story dressed in science fiction settings and characters and plots. Both genres had specific beats to hit, and not all beats agreed with each other. Every edit felt like a slight unravelling that led to bigger unravellings. The problems that kept on giving.

'Look,' Kip said, pointing at a page in the manuscript that was spread out on Brent's table. 'In this part, Amora is trying to establish that D:ECEMBE-R is an unreliable narrator. If you have two points of views, whatever it is she's trying to achieve with that isn't going to work.'

Of course, Emma wasn't going to let him win so easily. This was a major edit that she had fought him tooth and nail on in the past two weeks. 'If you take out too much of MAIA's point of view, then you take out the romance plot. All the emotional beats are in her chapters! Taking her out means taking out D:ECEMBE-R's humanity!'

'But the thematic question of this story is whether or not they've kept their humanity, and if it's worth keeping humanity given what they did to this planet.'

'What you're not getting is the story's fundamental theme!'

'What, pray tell, am I not getting, Morales? What is the story's fundamental theme?'

'Love!' she yelled, and only then did she notice just how quiet the office had become. She said the last part of her point quietly. 'And if love is a good enough reason to continue living. If the memory of a life lived in love makes living worth it.'

Kip was visibly stunned, his jaw dropping, his posture slack, hands at his side.

'Emma's right,' a girl's voice, all too familiar to Emma, said at the door. 'I mean I wasn't trying to get that exact message across. I just wanted to tell a story, but Emma saw where I was going. She always does even when I can't see it for myself yet.'

'Amora!' Brent was the first to the door, leading Amora to sit at the chair in front of his table. 'Thank you for coming to the office. This, as you know, is Kipling Alegre, managing editor, and Emma's co-editor for your latest book.'

Kip nodded to Amora and sat on the couch facing the desk behind the two chairs there.

Amora took off her face mask. 'I thought it best to talk to my editors in person about this new story, considering it's so different from my usual stuff.' She searched the room for Emma, curly hair bouncing off her shoulders, sharp eyes watery in the fluorescent light, uncomfortable being the centre of attention in the room.

Taking her cue, Emma took the chair next to Amora's. 'How much did you hear, Amora?'

'Enough. Was my manuscript bad, Emma?'

'It wasn't! It's your best work yet,' Emma said.

'It's not your best,' Kip said, propping his elbows on his knees so that he was leaning forward. 'Not yet.'

Amora looked to Emma before turning to Kip. Emma took Amora's hand and then stroked it with her thumb. Kip's brow arched, eyes on the gesture.

'Kip, let's talk in private later—' Kip shook his head and shot her a dark, strange look that cut her off mid-sentence.

'Amora, your story has so much potential, but it won't get there if we coddle you,' Kip said, switching glances between Amora and Emma, who was already standing. 'Let us help you create your best work yet.'

Emma glared at Kip, her blood boiling. How dare he insinuate that her methods were insufficient? 'Just because your authors don't like you, doesn't mean you get to undermine me in front of *my* author, Alegre.'

Alegre rose to his feet, matching Emma's dark glare and folding his arms across his chest. 'Don't take it personally, Morales. My methods get the best out of every book— and author.'

'And mine don't?' She stabbed her index finger at his chest. 'Is that what you're saying?'

'I'm saying you use too much heart when you should be using your head!'

'Is that why you insist on the robots?' She scoffed. 'You're a heartless robot yourself?'

'See! It always has to be personal with you—'

'Enough!' Brent ordered, standing up from his chair and passing a box of tissues to Amora.

Emma gasped and crouched so that she was eye to eye with her. 'This isn't about your work. You're fine . . .'

'Is the story so bad . . .' Amora said between sobs, barely getting the words out of her lips, hands on her face. 'That you two are fighting about it?'

'No, no, you're fine. Just our usual edits. Remember how we did it for your novellas?'

'This is nothing like your last book, Amora,' Kip said.

Emma rose to her feet and shoved Kip away. 'What is your problem?!'

Amora shot to her feet. 'Fine! I'll take back my story!'

Emma and Kip stood stunned then exchanged accusatory looks.

'Amora, this isn't—' Emma began to say.

'No, Emma, Mr Alegre is right. My manuscript is garbage.'

'It's not garbage,' Brent chimed in. 'Otherwise, we wouldn't be publishing it.'

'You can't stop me. I haven't signed a contract.'

Kip rolled his eyes, and Emma shoved him back again. 'Read the room, you jerk!'

Brent spoke up before Kip could retaliate, 'Both of you, out! Get out! I'll speak with Ms Romero alone.'

Kip gave Emma one more dark look before storming off. Emma patted Amora's shoulder on the way out, mouthing, 'Sorry,' as if one word could fix the problem.

***

Kip and Emma glared at each other, sitting at one of the tables nearest Brent's corner office. Given the right motivation, Emma could reach over the table, wrap her tiny hands around Kip's neck, and strangle him into submission.

The company had renovated the floor plan of the office to adapt to a more modern, digital workplace system, which when it was first proposed had sounded silly. Imagine applying digital-friendly innovations to an industry as traditional as book publishing.

Now, the open floor plan only provided an arena in which Emma could face Kip in a *Hating Game* style staring competition, which she was losing because she was distracted by the looks she was getting from their coworkers (and his dimples showing carelessly on his cheeks). Emma was sure everyone had heard them argue in front of the company's best-selling author, not to mention their boss.

Kip on the other hand looked unbothered by the attention with his arms folded across his chest and resting on the table and his face looking at her like he knew he was winning.

'You didn't have to humiliate me in front of Amora, you asshole,' Emma said, finally letting herself blink as she leaned back into her office chair and mimicked his posture.

'It wouldn't be humiliating if you didn't take this job too personally,' Kip said and then, sighing, shook his head. 'But you're right. I was out of line. I shouldn't have undermined you.'

Emma opened her lips expecting to argue with Kip again but found herself rendered speechless instead by Kip admitting defeat so quickly.

What was it that Janey had said— *Kip would have yielded to you, no problem.*'

She hadn't noticed it until now, but he did that all the time, making the knots in her stomach coil so tight that she could explode any minute, only to find no satisfaction of release save for her anticlimactic unravelling. It was like he knew exactly what to say and when to tie her in knots and then unravel her.

'I'm not saying it's bad to put your heart and soul in everything you do, but you've got to leave some for yourself. And you've got to leave room for others to fill themselves up with their own hearts and souls. You can't fix every problem by breaking off pieces of you.'

She frowned, maintaining intense eye contact with Kip. Something told her that this was meant to be about more than Amora's manuscript or work in general—perhaps even Nick, but she wasn't going to address that. She wasn't going to give him the satisfaction of knowing that he'd gotten under her skin. 'We were both assholes in there.'

'Agreed.'

'Amora doesn't respond to aggression well,' she said, fully uncoiling and relaxing in her chair, turning her head slightly to peek into Brent's office. 'It took her a long time to get over the last writer's block. Amora doesn't think she's doing legitimately good work because she's writing genre fiction.'

'Genre is an arbitrary classification of books so readers know where to go in a bookstore. It doesn't define quality, nor does it dictate what books readers will love.'

A corner of her lips quirked up. 'You plagiarized that from Neil Gaiman.'

'More like paraphrased, Buttercup.' He peeked into the room too.

She stared at him, trying to read him like a book. Kip was a far more experienced editor than she was, she had to admit that, but that didn't mean she didn't know her stuff. She'd been able to keep up with him in this ongoing book nerd-off. But then, maybe she was the only one who was taking the rivalry a tad too seriously. Kip had helped her in that confrontation with Nick, and Kip hadn't actually tried to take the project from her. He'd even talked Brent into allowing a co-editor setup for this project.

In fact, he seemed hurt when she'd all but said that he was terrible to his authors.

Maybe she was taking their little rivalry too seriously. Perhaps there was a way for them to work on this manuscript without fighting like children in a schoolyard.

'If, by some miracle of the universe, Amora decides to sign over her story to us, we need to find a better way to collaborate.'

This time, she had the pleasure of seeing him unravel, his tense shoulders slacking, his arms unfolding, his face softening for her. Then he grinned in that self-satisfied way that rattled her. Every. Freaking. Time. 'You still want my help?'

'Don't flatter yourself, Alegre,' she said, rolling her eyes. 'But I admit that I do need your expertise. Amora's a great writer, but she gets in too deep in her head sometimes, especially when she's trying something new. But she shines when she gets out of her comfort zone. I know what I'm good at, and I understand that I'd only be doing her a disservice by not giving her the best. So, if you still want a hand in this—'

'I'll do it,' he said without preamble, cutting her off mid-sentence.

She raised an index finger, both to reprimand him for interrupting her and to take back control. 'I have conditions.'

'Name them.'

'One, all your edits go through me, and you don't talk to Amora directly. You intimidate her, which doesn't help her write faster.'

'Done.'

'Two, you let me give you a deep dive on what romance is, to help you better understand where my edits are coming from.'

'Let me guess. Next, you'll tell me I'm not allowed to fall in love with you?'

She scowled at him, her jaw clenching. She stood to leave, saying, 'If you're not going to take this seriously—'

'Fine!' Kip said, standing to grab her wrist from across the table and gently pulling her to sit back down. 'But only if you let me give you a deep dive into what science fiction and fantasy are, to help you better understand where my edits are coming from.'

She narrowed her eyes at him, suspicious and intrigued. This was a bad idea, and she sensed that this would be the source of this story arc's dramatic tension. Heck, this whole deal between them felt like a trope from a romance comedy. But Emma was a book lover, and books had never failed her or lied to her. So, against her better judgement—or maybe because of it, she said, 'Deal.'

Chapter 8

Magic

Kip's first lesson was magic.

He was going to explain to her what magic systems were and how they worked in a story structure so that he would finally shut up about it when they argued about *Menagerie*'s story structure.

'How could there be magic in this? It's science fiction!' Emma asked after the nth time he kept saying no to all her edits because, quote, ' . . . laws of magic.'

'Magic makes the impossible possible if it were in the real world,' Kip said as he loaded files into the proofing machine. 'Say you want to bend this pen with your mind.' He raised a pen up to her face—the sleeves of his shirt riding up his shapely arms—and wiggled it between his thumb and index finger. 'If you actually use magic, it'll bend like a rubber band without you needing to touch it. If you use tools like a saw, you're using technology.'

Emma smiled at him, her face downcast, but her eyes looking up at him through thick black lashes like she had a dumb plan in her stupid head that she was dying to execute.

'I know how to do it without magic or technology.' Emma grabbed the pen, tried to bend its plastic body, and ended up cracking the plastic into two, the ink-filled straw and spring spilling to the floor and staining her left palm black. 'There. Just elbow grease.' She shook the dripping ink off her hands. 'And a lot of ink.' *Okay, so this was a really stupid plan.*

'That's cheating, and you didn't technically bend it. You broke it.' He took out a white handkerchief from his pocket and held out his free hand to her. The action startled her into just giving her ink-stained left hand to him without question.

'All this to prove a point,' Kip said, moving to dab the cloth on her palm.

She pulled away her hand just before he reached her palm. 'No! The ink will never wash off!'

Kip clicked his tongue and grabbed her hand again, gently wiping the ink off her palm. 'It's just a handkerchief.' He stopped when she cringed and hissed in pain. The simple movement of pulling her hand up close to his face—so close that he was practically breathing on her fingertips, the tips close to his slightly parted lips as his tongue slid along the lower lip—made her forget why she'd cringed for a moment. 'And you're bleeding, too.' He pulled out a small shard of plastic from the pad of her palm, and suddenly the sharp sting was back. Kip then pulled out a small bottle of ethyl alcohol from his pocket and sprayed it all over her palm without warning.

This time, she cursed, 'Mother of bejeezus!' trying and failing to jerk her hand away from his grip. 'Are you punishing me, Dolores Umbridge?'

He arched an eyebrow at her, momentarily looking up from wiping off the watered-down ink and blood still on her palm. 'For what, Harry Potter? Not believing in magic?' He put away the handkerchief and examined her hand again. 'Go wash your hand with soap and water. The rest of the ink should come off.' But he didn't let go of her hand just yet. Instead, he looked up at her, his head tilting upwards like the world was in slow motion until his eyes met hers, and they were still holding hands. He closed his big, rough hand around her smaller one, the warmth of it surging up her arms and into her heart, which bloomed into an explosion of heat in her body. He squeezed, eyes never breaking contact with hers through his thick dark-rimmed glasses, his lips parting open and pressing close and parting open again like he was short of breath.

Emma felt herself leaning in long enough to realize what she had intended to do. 'I should go to the washroom.'

He cleared his throat and let go of her hand like it was hot coal. 'Right, right, before it gets infected.' He turned away from her so abruptly that she wondered if it was because he was trying to hide his blushing face or if the proofer had cut the proof of the pages he had loaded into it a moment ago.

***

She rejoined him at the table they shared in the open office space, sitting right across from him, a pile of proofs, printouts, and paperwork that neither of them remembered ever using or needing between them.

'So, uhm . . . magic?'

He looked up from the pile of proofs he was checking. 'Wha—What? What magic?'

'You were talking about magic before . . . you know . . . ' Whatever that was.

'Right, right, magic and magic systems. *Menagerie*'s magic system follows hard rules for it to work, and Amora has been inconsistent with the rules she set when MAIA and D:ECEMBE-R use the magic.'

'It's still not clear to me what magic is in this setup. Isn't magic, by nature, supposed to be infinite? If you enforce rules and limits on it, then doesn't that make . . . *not* magic?'

'Ah, Arthur C. Clark and Isaac Asimov said something similar. "Sufficiently advanced technology is indistinguishable from magic," and when "magic must abide by rules and respect limits, then it is no longer magic; it is merely exotic technology." Which only goes to show that the magic (and science) can be more science-y or fantastical depending on the story.'

'So, you just want consistency in the magic system of this story? That's it?'

'More than that, Amora used the magic to solve some of the major obstacles that MAIA and D:ECEMBE-R encounter throughout the story, thereby manipulating the story structure in a way that feels unsatisfying.' He rifled through the pile of paper on the table space between them and pulled out a relatively clean sheet of paper. He drew a line across the sheet and wrote the words 'soft' and 'hard' on either end of the line. 'Brandon Sanderson, in my mind the greatest science fiction and fantasy author of all time, popularized the three laws of magic in worldbuilding and creating magic systems in science fiction and fantasy settings. Sanderson's first law: An author's ability to solve conflict with magic is directly proportional to how well the reader understands said magic.' He pointed at the end marked 'hard'. 'The closer the magic is here, the more the laws must apply to it. Here.' He pointed to the end marked 'soft'. 'The closer the magic is to this point, meaning it can't be explained nor does it follow a strict set of rules, the less the laws apply, and the less it should be used to solve problems in the story.'

As he continued to talk about Sanderson's laws, all her mind could process was just how jacked he was. She has only known him as the SFF nerd who wore nerdy glasses and nerdy shirts and had the dorkiest, most adorable smile she had ever

seen on a person in her six years in the company. He looked
so much different before the lockdown. He filled out his nerd
shirts more now than he did back then. She remembered the
first time she'd seen him in the lobby of the office when she
was only interviewing for a junior editor position. He was only
a junior editor then, and the managing editor at the time, Lily,
was the one who'd interviewed her.

Emma had been reading *The Princess Bride* that day, a very
thick fantasy tome that she regretted bringing to a job interview
to read, as she waited for Lily to come into the office. She'd
arrived with Kip, who'd weirdly engaged Emma in an awkward
staring contest before walking further into the offices.

She liked to think that that was when their stupid game
began, because the day after she was hired, he'd asked her
which version of *The Princess Bride* she liked more, the book or
the movie.

'Earth to Bridget Jones?' He waved a hand in front of her
eyes. 'Earth to Bridget Jones? Are you there?'

She scowled, narrowing his eyes at him. 'Are you calling
me ditzy?'

'Hey, Bridget Jones is far from ditzy,' Kip said like he was
proud of the reference.

'Wow. Never took you for a rom-com junkie,' Emma said,
looking over the sheet of paper he had been scribbling on
and seeing that he had written a bunch of names from SFF
literature along the line. Had she really spent all that time just
thinking about how jacked Kip had become?

'What? I like rom-coms, and I'm not ashamed to admit
it,' Kip said, shaking his head and going back to working on
his proofs.

And that just made her laugh. *'Bridget Jones's Diary* is a good
movie. It's just so random coming from you.'

He shrugged. 'I like what I like. By the way, you're pulling an all-nighter again, are you?'

'How'd you know?'

'You loaded an entire book into the machine. The proofing paper ran out while you were in the bathroom. Wait—' he said, stopping her as she stood up. 'I already replaced the roll and reloaded your files. It won't be done until tomorrow morning so you should go home now.'

'No, I should stay. Just to make sure that it doesn't stop midway. You know how prickly the machine can get. I live nearby anyway. Don't you live far away? Maybe you should go home.'

'Nah, I want to be done with my round tonight so the artists can have a go at these piles first thing tomorrow morning. I'll stay and watch the machine.'

She frowned at him. 'Admit it, you want to stay so you can snoop around our stuff and do weird shit all over the office.'

He smirked, studying her face like he was trying to solve a math equation, like two plus two is five. 'What kind of weird shit were you thinking, you sicko?'

'I don't know. Hide all the staplers. Poop in the ladies' washroom. Run around naked and sit bare-assed on all the office chairs.'

'Yes, yes, I intend to run around naked and stick my naked butt all over the office, starting with your favourite chair.' He pointed at her chair. 'That one.'

'Mean,' she said, her mouth opening to do a weird combination of a laugh and another yawn.

Kip was trying and failing to stifle a laugh. 'Go home, Morales. You look like shit.'

She faked a gasp. 'So mean!' He watched her pack up her things. 'Are you sure about this? You can message me if something happens to the proofer again. I can run back here to fix it.'

'I'm perfectly capable of handling a fifteen-year-old proofing machine, thank you very much. Go home. I'll text you when I'm in distress.'

'And you call me Buttercup.' She slung her bag over her shoulder uncertainly, switching glances between the door and Kip just waiting for her to leave. 'Just leave the proofs in the basket when they're done printing. I'll cut them when I get here tomorrow morning.'

'It won't be me doing the cutting. It'll be the ghosts. Or I could do it with just my mind. Like magic.'

She rolled her eyes, yawned, and waved goodbye to Kip. 'Bye, Hobbit.'

'Bye, Buttercup,' he said, watching her walk out the glass doors.

The next morning, her proofs were on her table, neatly cut and organized by page.

Just like magic.

Chapter 9

Meet-cute

There was an art and science to the meet-cute.

On the one hand, the meet-cute was the nexus from which an epic of two hearts began. It was where lovers finally gravitated together and built the beginnings of the orbit by which their lives circled and circled and circled till the end of time or till the inevitable demise of their star system's sun.

It had certainly felt like that with Nick, the first time Emma laid her eyes on him six years ago, the bad boy in the leather jacket on the motorcycle riding up to the bar—a place that Emma had no business being in, given the mountain of work she'd left at the office. He was smoking and drinking, losing himself to the music in the pit of bodies dancing and gyrating and grinding with each other, while Emma had to be physically pushed into the mosh pit by Janey, who was trying to get to the DJ. Their eyes had met from across the room, and their bodies had met in the black hole of people too far gone in the night to see what was about to transpire between her and him—the big bang. A new galaxy was born. Nick and Emma's galaxy.

On the other hand, the meet-cute was only a promise of what was to come and not necessarily the life that must come after—a lesson carved so deeply into her bones these past six years.

Nevertheless, her meet-cute with Nick, it was art and poetry and science rolled into one.

This meet-cute Janey was trying to orchestrate with the cute gym coach, this felt more like torture—at least for Emma. Janey seemed to be having the time of her life.

Now that she was thinking about it, it seemed fitting— oh the poetic justice!—to physically torture herself with this impromptu CrossFit class after a gruelling week of trying to work with Kip Alegre. Not that she'd willingly choose CrossFit over sitting comfy at her desk at home in her ratty *pambahay* after today. She'd forgotten why she agreed to this in the first place.

'Tell me again why you made me do this, Janey? I can't remember. Even my brain feels dead,' Emma said between painful breaths after the evening class.

'You needed to release some of that tension that's obviously eating you up from the inside, Ems,' Janey said, jogging in place while Emma lay on the black rubber-padded ground, willing her legs to get up and go and failing. She couldn't care less about the years of sweat soaked into the mat. She lived here now. 'I gave you the choice between getting laid with a stranger you meet at a bar and CrossFit. Now, here we are.' She said the last part with a grin and an ostentatious wave of her hands, pointing at the gym, her face smug and the words 'You made your choice' sparkling behind her eyes.

'We could have done other things, you know. I hear board game cafés are making a comeback. And breakout rooms,' Emma said. 'And I didn't think I was *that* stressed, not enough to want this.' Kip had been more pleasant to work with than she'd expected. It was the deadlines that were killing her and the impending loss of a job she loved so much.

Emma sat up, despite every muscle of her body screaming at her not to, her once-neat ponytail in disarray all over her sweaty, sticky face and back and shoulders.

Janey picked up their matching water bottles, pink and green, and handed the green one to Emma. 'As your best friend, I'm obligated to tell you that you are definitely *that* stressed.' She drank from her bottle and made eyes with their coach who was busy putting the equipment bank on the racks, clearly smiling at and distracted by Janey. 'You and Alegre were bumming everyone out at the office.'

Emma groaned, rolled her eyes, and lay back down on the floor, covering her eyes with her forearms. 'Not this again, Janey.'

'Come on. You never complain about the manuscripts that land in your inbox—not even the one you had to practically rewrite from scratch—'

Eyes still covered, Emma pointed at her friend, 'That's supposed to be confidential, Ms January Flores!'

'Whatever! Point is, you never say no to any job. You never complain about how bad a manuscript is. And you never complain about a hundred authors making demands of you. You just sit there stewing at your desk till the work is done. Because that's who you are. You fix problems. You do the work. But with *Menagerie*? You just lose your marbles? No way.'

Emma took her arm off her eyes and glared at her friend, her contact lenses slightly askew and eyeballs beginning to feel dry. Janey was batting her eyelashes at the coach who was responding super well to her flirtations.

'*Menagerie* is the biggest manuscript of my career!' Emma said, sitting up and making Janey look at her. 'And you heard what Brent said, we need it to succeed if we want to stay employed!'

'No, I think it's Alegre. He's gotten under your skin, more than the usual.' Janey grinned, eyes downcast in a conspiratorial look directed at Emma. 'It eats you up that someone else is able to fix a problem that you can't.' Janey stood up and offered a hand to help her best friend up. Emma just glared at her open palm, debating in her head if it was truly worth the pain of standing up. 'Admit it, Emma, you're much too competitive for your own good.'

In the past week, Emma and Kip had been at each other's throats with *Menagerie*, slowly and, most of the time, painfully cutting down each of their fifty pages of edits to one shared online drive file that somehow made sense. In the past two weeks, they'd argued in the office, in video meetings, in emails, in text messages, in chats, in calls—in just about every avenue they met, they'd fought. Neither of them was happy with that shared file, and they were already a week late in sending their edits back to Amora. They were supposed to hash it out one last time today, which was why she'd left the comfort of her home for the fifth time this week. They'd just ended up fighting again.

And it couldn't have come at a worse time for either of them. He had his Summer Komikon books for submission to the printer at the end of the month, and she was at the tail end, the proofing stage, in the process of finalizing her Valentine's Day books. For five days in a row, they had had to come to the office to work from morning till late, late night, stopping only to get food, go to the bathroom, or glare at each other when their minds were running on fumes. They were tired, tense, and furious. No wonder they were powder kegs just waiting to explode any minute—a thing that her best friend was able to curtail before Emma and Kip literally blew up the office together.

Why did it have to be with CrossFit? Damn it.

Emma pouted and took her friend's hand, which pulled her up so quickly and forcefully that she let out an ugly groan of pain, echoing in the emptying gym.

'This is your fault, Janey,' Emma said, patting her sore lower back. 'And I am not *that* competitive. I just don't like leaving problems unsolved. It makes me itchy.'

But her friend's attention wasn't on her any more. Their coach was done dicking around with the equipment and had finally worked up the nerve to approach Janey.

This was a problem that Emma could solve for her best friend. 'Welp, I have more proofs waiting to be cut and checked at the office.' Not to mention the Balrog-incarnate waiting to argue with Emma again about *Menagerie*, but she wasn't going to tell her friend that. Janey took her hand in hers and squeezed, saying 'thank you' and 'love you' wordlessly with her eyes as the coach approached.

'See you tomorrow, Janey.' She patted her friend's shoulder and limped away, resisting the urge to cry out in pain with every step and dreading seeing Kip again. Unlike Janey's meet-cute with the coach, this meeting with Kip wasn't going to be cute.

Maybe she did prefer CrossFit to facing off with Kip again, she thought and changed her mind when she got to the office.

It was after office hours. Everyone had gone home already, so the floor was empty save for her lone laptop near the proofing machine, which was turned off. She had loaded her files into the machine before Janey had dragged her away, but the basket was empty.

She looked under, over, and behind—nothing. Did her proofs not print? She turned to her desk and saw the proofs there, cut, sorted, and placed neatly next to her laptop. He'd done it again. Did he get a kick out of using the cutting board?

On the screen of her laptop was a sticky note that said:

'*No one is happy. So, it must be a good compromise. I yield to you, Tyrion Lannister. ~K*'

She found she wasn't completely unhappy. Just unravelled. Again. This was becoming a habit of his, catching her by surprise, and she'd care if only her real muscles weren't actually so tense and twisted up in knots.

Chapter 10

Valentine's Day

Emma supposed that Valentine's Day would be as good a time as any to give Kip a lesson on Romance, but the coincidence of it made her shudder. It was so coincidental that any self-respecting book editor would think twice about it. She thought, *Come on? Romance lessons on Valentine's Day? The cliché! Gasp!*

Instead, she went to the office to help Janey in the pre-event prep for the Valentine's Day book launch that night. The theme was prom, featuring the four new books that Emma had been working on for months. While Janey was a flurry of activity alone—making calls, texting, and chatting, making notes on her tablet, and ordering interns and hired help around, Emma, Kip, and Jesse were filling loot bags with books, merchandise, and postcards. The art department was busy with event decorations, circulations and accounting with inventory—many of them getting ready to leave for the venue.

'I feel like an Oompa Loompa right now,' Jesse said, as she stored finished loot bags into boxes. Jesse was a fresh grad from one of the university-belt schools, and she had an accent that made Emma twist her tongue and feel so very old. The kid was good, but she was yet to shed off the blind passion and naïve optimism that came with youth. Gen Z was Emma's favourite generation.

'Get used to doing five jobs at a time if you want to stay in this industry, kid,' Kip said, walking down the line of bags on the table and dropping books in them. 'Traditional publishing in a country that can't afford books is like wearing a sweater to the beach. It might look nice. It might save you from sunburn, but it's sure as heck uncomfortable.'

'Don't listen to Captain Oompa Loompa there, Jesse.' Emma glared and shook her head at Kip, who shrugged, the arm carrying stacks of books flexing as he moved. 'Filipinos are readers. Otherwise, we'd have been out of a job years ago.'

'But won't that be the case for us next year?' Jesse asked, taping down one box. 'If you two don't deliver that manuscript?'

Emma and Kip exchanged looks, urging the other to answer. She hadn't heard back from Amora yet about the proposed edits that they'd sent her more than a week ago. There had been radio silence all throughout, and though it was normal not to get feedback immediately on a manuscript revision, Emma still fretted as more days went by without word from Amora.

'It's not just the one manuscript, kid. Every book we make counts for the bottom line,' Kip said when Emma took too long to answer. 'And even if we don't make it—and I'm not saying that we won't, most of us are still here because we like making books, isn't that right, Morales?'

Before Emma could answer, she was distracted by a delivery man carrying a bouquet of sunflowers in the lobby.

'Emma?' Kip followed her line of sight and saw the delivery man take the flowers to her.

Janey ran to him. 'I didn't order flowers!' she yelled, trying to stop him. Kip turned his back on the scene, aiming to get more books to slip into the bags.

'These are for a Ms Emma Morales,' the delivery guy said, turning his attention to Emma who absently accepted the flowers. 'From a Mr Nick.'

'What does *he* want?' Janey asked and, concerned by the sudden sour expression on Emma's face, grabbed the flowers from Emma and read the note.

Emma read the note herself while Janey returned the flowers to the delivery man. 'Send it back. We don't want it.'

'*Friendly flowers from a friend? Happy Valentine's Day, Ems. ~Nick,*' the note said, sending visceral surges of lightning through her veins. Jesse helped her into a seat. Emma watched the flowers walk away from her and out of the office.

'Jesse, get the interns to help you take these boxes into the van,' Janey said, pulling a chair to sit next to Emma. Jesse did as she was told, and Janey took Emma's trembling hands in hers and said, 'Well, fuck.' Janey always knew what to say to make others feel good around her, and for her to decide that nothing but 'Well, fuck,' was the appropriate response for this, while her phone and tablet beeped incessantly, was jarring for Emma.

Janey looked like she was ready to drop everything for her best friend, but Emma stopped her before she did anything that could get her fired. 'I'm fine, Janey. Go to your event. I'll stay and get some work done before I go home.'

Her best friend stared at her like she didn't believe her, but the beeping had escalated to call ringtones. 'Swear to me that we'll talk about this tomorrow.'

Emma squeezed her hands. 'Of course, I'm legally obligated to tell you everything, right? Now go,' she said, gently but firmly prodding Janey off the chair and away. Janey gave Emma one last concerned look, her body divided between dropping everything for her and leaving Emma behind when she needed a friend, before practically dragging herself away while barking orders at everyone to move out. 'Let's get this over with, people!'

Emma was left alone with the note on her lap, Nick's familiar handwriting making her squeamish.

'I never liked giving bouquets of flowers,' Kip said as he dropped the last book into the last bag, which he packed into the box.

'What?' Emma stared at him blankly.

'When you pluck a flower from the stem, it begins to die,' Kip said, picking up the box to take to the lobby, the move lifting up his shirt—a *Red Rising* propaganda fan shirt in black with red and gold print this time, with the words *'Live for more'* emblazoned in crimson text on the front— slightly so that she caught a glimpse of skin. 'I can't imagine a more aggressive message to send to a lover than "I love you so much, I'd rather you die in my arms than live without me."'

'All right, Alegre. What would you give a girl?'

'Something alive ideally. Like a potted plant or better yet a cactus.'

He walked away before she could finish saying 'How romantic.'

She hadn't realized that she was crumpling the note in her hand till a sharp end dug deep into her palm where her cut had almost healed completely. It wasn't the flowers really that unsettled her, but rather who sent them and the intention behind it. She knew that Nick meant exactly what he said in the note, but like everything about Nick, it was laced with something dark and vicious. Nick was a creature who lived like every day was trying to cut him down, and their entire relationship had been about helping him up every time he fell. It took such a toll on Emma that she'd barely recognized herself when finally, she'd ended it. Nick was an unsolved problem that she'd abandoned. Nick was an unsolved problem she did not know how to fix. Nick was a problem she'd left behind when she'd felt like she was drowning.

'Well, they're all gone,' Kip said, startling her from her thoughts.

Emma looked around the empty office like she'd woken up from a dream and then stood up mechanically, ready to leave this day behind. She dropped the note on the desk and wordlessly moved to pack up her things, two tables over.

'Days like this, editors are better off staying out of everybody's way,' he said, packing up his things, surreptitiously stealing a glance at the crumpled note, and then approaching her. 'I suppose today's as good a day as any for that lesson in romance, Jane Austen.'

She stared at him, unsure if she heard him right, and then laughed out loud.

'It is Valentine's Day after all,' she said.

***

'So, a romance is a love story,' Emma said as they pulled into the airport parking lot, already regretting her decision to go here when Kip asked where she wanted to 'conduct her lesson'.

'I know that, Buttercup,' Kip said, backing into a free spot that gave them the perfect view of the airport and the aeroplanes lifting off into the night sky. 'Give me more credit than that.'

Emma rolled her eyes, only this time it was in jest. Kip had been quiet the entire ride, and oddly, being around him didn't feel as antagonistic today as it usually did.

'All romances are love stories, but not all love stories are romances,' Emma said.

'Explain,' Kip said, reaching into the glove compartment, his arm merely inches from her, and taking out a Ziploc bag of trail mix containing nuts, dried berries, and dried vegetables. He opened the bag and offered it to her.

Emma gave it a disgusted look, which made him laugh. 'Come on. It would do you good to eat something healthy for once.'

'How do you know what I eat in a day, Hobbit?'

'Last week, I watched you eat cup noodles and MILKY WAY for lunch five days in a row, Buttercup.'

'Okay, personal space, Humbert Humbert,' Emma said, pushing the trail mix back to him.

'Lucky for you,' he said, placing the bag on his lap and reaching into the glove compartment again, the scent of his shampoo wafting up Emma's nose, the scent of musk and spice and mint mixed with his own scent after a day's work, 'I keep candy bars in here, too.' He passed her a MILKY WAY chocolate bar, which she grabbed out of his hand.

'I never took you for a health buff,' Emma said after biting into the chocolate bar.

His hand was in the trail mix. 'Only after the breakup.'

Emma gasped. 'You had a girlfriend?' she practically screamed, candy bar midway to her mouth.

He frowned, looking partly offended and partly amused. 'Don't look so surprised! I have a life outside of work, you know.'

She bit into the candy bar. 'You just spend so much time in the office. You practically live there. When did you even get the time to date?'

'Honestly, I think that was part of the problem,' he said, sighing and leaning back into his chair, averting his eyes from her. 'She fell in love with someone else—or rather fell back in love with her ex—while I was busy working.'

This was the most that Kip had told her in all the time they'd been working together. Who knew that he was going through a breakup?

'Did you try to win her back? How are you fine after that?'

'I did, but she made sure it was a clean break. We're friends actually. I'll be *ninong* to their first child.' He pulled out his phone and brought out the picture of an infant held in its mother's arms. She caught a glimpse of a wedding band on the mother's ring finger: a white gold vine-style wedding band with small diamonds embedded into the metal. She was captivated by it, and tried to remember where she had seen that ring design before but got distracted by the wistful look that fell on Kip's face when he looked at the photo on the phone. It was gone before Emma could pinpoint if it was the sad kind of wistful. 'Anyway, what are we doing here?' he asked, tucking the phone back into his pocket. 'Are we going somewhere for this big romance lesson of yours? Is this a *Casablanca* situation?'

'More like *Love Actually*. I thought it was a good idea when I suggested it at first, but I'm starting to think otherwise.'

'But we're just in the parking lot, Buttercup.'

'I'm too broke to buy tickets just to get us on a plane or inside the airport, Hobbit.'

'We're not very good at this real-life romance thing, are we, Buttercup?' he said with a sheepish laugh, fingers drumming on the wheel like he was working up the nerve to say something else. Instead, he said, 'Okay, what's the lesson?'

'Happy endings. Romances are love stories that always, and I mean always, have happy endings.'

'Like *Sleepless in Seattle*, *The Wedding Singer*, and *Crazy Rich Asians* are romance stories, and *Casablanca* is a love story, but not a romance?'

'Exactly!' She stopped to give him a curious stare. 'It still surprises me how many rom-coms you watch.'

'I may not know how to edit romance novels, but I am hopelessly romantic.'

'You're not so hopeless. You had a girlfriend.'

'Ex-girlfriend. I guess we'll find out soon enough how hopeless I am, won't we?' He trailed off on the last part like he'd realized that he hadn't meant to say it out loud midway but then decided to finish it anyway.

She paid it no heed for now, deciding he must be embarrassed to talk about a past failed relationship. 'Anyway' she said with a weird intonation that intended to break away from the topic before it got awkward but ended up being awkward anyway. 'This is why we can't move the ending to an earlier point where it's unclear that D:ECEMBE-R and MAIA end up together.'

He had that faraway look again, the crease between his brows deepening, his posture tense and tightening as if straining to pull at a rope. 'If that's the case, I think Amora should build up that last scene where they meet again at the space station. Rather than ending it right where they see each other up there, there should be a scene where they physically reunite. And an epilogue of what happens to them after the last chapter.'

Emma clapped in agreement, her face bright with joy. 'Yes! Yes! Now you're getting it!'

The corner of his lip quirked upward in that same unironic, genuine smile that made her stomach twist in knots a little bit, the dimples dipping on either side of his cheek. She patted his forearm, his eyes following her hand there, 'If I knew that this was how we understand each other's processes, I would have forced you to do this with me earlier on. Would've saved us a lot of grief.'

'You always sound so surprised when I hint at a rudimentary understanding of love and romance. I'm beginning to think that you actually believe I'm a heartless robot.'

'It's not the genre. It's you. You always look so effortlessly—clinically, sociopathically even . . . put-together.'

'I don't know what you mean by that, but nothing I do is effortless. Not compared to you. You're independent. You're good at what you do. If there's anybody I know who's put-together, it's you.'

She felt her face warm up, and she resisted the urge to cover her for-sure red cheeks. 'Thanks.' Suddenly, every nerve, every feeling she had was projected on her hand that was resting on his forearm, and it felt like pulling away a bag of rocks when she let go. They looked at each other, unsure now of what to do next, say next. Outside, planes took to the skies, filling the air with the zoom and boom of machines taking people everywhere. Meanwhile, Emma and Kip stayed here, hearts drumming in their ears, breaths mingling in this small, shared space, lives intertwining at this nexus in time. The big bang. A star exploding. A new galaxy was being born.

Kip cleared his throat, averting his gaze. 'Guys can like romance, too, Buttercup. We're past that age when romance is exclusively female.'

Emma tried not to sigh loudly, happy that she wasn't the one to break the spell, but also oddly disappointed that it had to end. 'A point that you have so clearly proven with your expansive knowledge of the genre,' she said in an effort to sound flippant.

'Damn straight,' he said, fidgeting with the wheel, drumming his fingers on it, then compulsively reaching for his bag of trail mix before changing his mind and going back to holding on to the wheel, this time with a vice-like grip. Then he trained his eyes on her, serious and fearful, ardent and hopeful, as if it took him so much energy to say the next words out of his mouth. 'I don't suppose today's happy ending ends with both of us getting dinner.'

She laughed. 'If I didn't know better, you Hobbit, I'd think you're asking me out on a date,' she joked, realizing too late that this wasn't just their usual banter.

'Well, it is Valentine's Day, Princess Buttercup,' he said unironically.

Chapter 11

Clean Break

This day in March would fall on a fine spring day if this were an American romance. The sun was out, and it was warm. Not the prickly, burning kind of summer warmth, but cool, like the soft touch of a warm blanket in a cold room. Everything was alive, newly awakened from the long dream of winter. Spring was the promise of a new beginning, new lives, new loves.

In the Philippines, this day was crazy hot. Emma was sweating through her floral cotton dress under the merciless tropical sun as she made her way to a quaint café in that hip new foodie district in the south. It was one of those places with the fancy names for coffee and dim incandescent lighting over black metal and dark wood interiors and furnishing.

It was all so very romantic if only this were a date. But it was not.

The AC blasting against her face upon entry was a cool reprieve from the heat outside, drying the sweat on her face and making her sweat-soaked dress colder against her already cold skin. She'd be shivering soon enough. Her phone had been vibrating relentlessly with messages from Janey telling her to send updates every minute on the minute just so she knew Emma was still alive. *She's exaggerating,* Emma thought. Janey had once told Emma that Nick exuded serial-killer energy—in front of Nick's face.

Still, she opened her phone to message her best friend. She saw a message from Kip, and a smile crept up her face and a warmth ebbed in the pit of her stomach. 'Good morning, Buttercup. Morning without you is a dwindling dawn.'

They've moved on from literary banter—because honestly, at this point, neither denied that the other knew books, and no one was really winning their game—to who could give the best quotes from literature out of context.

She replied with, 'Do you wish me a good morning, or mean that it is a good morning whether I want it or not; or that you feel good this morning; or that it is a morning to be good on?'

'Ah, I do love Tolkien in the morning.'

'Kinda dark greeting me with Dickinson, Hobbit.'

'I know you liked it, Buttercup,' he retorted. She shook her head, grinning uncontrollably, and tucked her phone back into her pocket.

She spotted Nick immediately, sitting on a bar stool in front of the elevated table, a binder of sheet music open in front of him, hot coffee to the side, and his head ducked low as he read. His arms were folded over the table, flexed in a way that stretched the artwork tattoos on his arms. He looked up as if sensing her gravitational pull there. She sensed it, too, and she had half the mind to run away. She didn't.

She sat on the stool across from him and smiled. He smiled back, all the hard parts of him softening at the sight of her.

'I thought you weren't coming,' he said, closing the book in front of him. 'Do you want coffee?' He moved to get off the chair, but she stopped him.

It was strange sitting in front of Nick now, and seeing a stranger when once upon a time, she had slept with her cheeks on his chest, his arms around her on the hood of his car under a night sky. It was an impromptu trip to Tagaytay, back before the pandemic, and she'd asked him if he'd like to see the shooting stars racing across the sky that night. And he'd asked her to be his girlfriend that night. And she'd said yes.

Back in the coffee shop, neither knew what to do next, where to start, why they were trying to do this.

'How have you been, Emma?' he asked, a distant, wistful sound lacing the tone of his voice. She could tell it was loaded with far more meaning, more questions that had once poured so easily out of his lips.

'I'm fine, Nick,' she said, avoiding his gaze. She remembered why she was here. A clean break. Like the kind Kip had with his ex. She could do that. Maybe she should have asked Kip what he meant by a 'clean break', or how his ex had done it, but then it would have felt like rubbing salt on an open wound. Kip didn't seem like he was totally over the woman. 'How have you been?' she asked, as if she didn't catch glimpses of his life online and from common friends.

He'd lost a lot of weight since they'd broken up, and he'd gotten a haircut, too. He'd been singing new songs at the bar where he played gigs with his band. They were all new songs—breakup songs, love songs, confused songs, angry songs. A month after their breakup, he'd posted an intimate picture with a woman, Abby, the bartender who worked in the same bar. He didn't post another photo after that, and the woman untagged herself from it and even unfriended him soon after.

He answered her honestly, sincerely, earnestly. Like months hadn't passed since they'd last seen each other. And it was like old times, when all was good between them, and they hadn't drifted apart, and they saw each other almost every day no matter what. It was like all the pain they had inflicted on each other hadn't happened.

But all of it did happen. Their love was a slow painful death that she had to end before they wasted away in each other's lives. Nick needed a lover who would be there for him all the time. And Emma needed one who understood that she needed a life apart from him, from the thing that was *them* so she could be *her*. *There were many different ways to kill the one you love. The slowest way was never loving them enough.* And it wasn't so easy to shrug off.

Maybe that would always be the case between former lovers. There would always be a flame there burning still, diminishing over time, but never snuffing out. She still cared about Nick, that much she would admit to herself. Maybe a clean break was acknowledging that there were still embers there, looking back at it fondly and thinking it was once good and it was once a raging fire burning them both.

There was still a soft spot for Nick in her life, she knew, and when it was her turn to talk about what she'd been up to since their breakup, she just told him everything, the way very dear childhood friends could slot back into each other's lives so easily after decades apart.

'I'm sorry about your mother, Emma,' Nick said, taking her hand from across the table. 'I should have been there for you when you needed me.'

Surprisingly, she didn't let go of his hand. 'It was the pandemic. A lot was going on for all of us.'

'Still, I should have been there. For you. I could still be that person for you.'

This time, she did break their touch, slipping out of his hand sharply like needles had pricked her skin within his hold. 'Nick . . . '

'I know. I know. All we can be now is friends.' He breathed in deeply like it hurt to say the words. 'I can live with friends. We were friends before we became lovers, weren't we?'

This was good, right? Exes could be friends, right? This was what she wanted all along. She was friends with her ex, like Kip was friends with his. The clean break. Well, clean enough.

The thought of Kip pulled her away from this café to that crowded fast-food place near the airport because no other place good enough for a date had had seats available. It was Valentine's Day after all. It was far from the perfect date and so far from their place of work. She and Kip had spent the night talking about books and movies and stories over burgers and fries. She couldn't stop the smile blooming on her face. The memory was a comfortable kind of warmth, like a warm blanket in a cold room.

'Yes. Friends,' she said, another fire began to burn in her, overpowering an old ember that still lived there and refused to die.

Chapter 12

The Road of Trials

'At some point in the story, the hero's mettle is tested,' Kip said as he and Emma joined their team's huddle right before the obstacle course started.

They were in an obstacle course park—'The biggest obstacle course park in the world!' was emblazoned on the archway over the entrance—which was a three-hour drive from the city. The representatives from the other companies under the umbrella conglomerate were already warming up in the waiting area when Maya Press joined them, the hot summer sun bearing down on all of them, browning and tanning skins all around. Emma had to wipe the sweat off her brow with the hem of her sleeveless Maya Press jersey shirt.

Even before they got here, Kip and Emma's attention had been on each other, almost forgetting that much of the day's activities relied on them. They had begun a discussion of mythologies as prototypes and precursors for most modern storytelling in the bus going here, and, somehow it had turned into an argument on how the monomyth applied to the standard romance story arc as they were putting on safety gear. They got so into the debate that when they looked up, their teammates were already at the starting point of the obstacle course and they had to run there. Kip, of course, was still running his mouth on the way, and for some reason, Emma thought of other ways that mouth could be put to good use.

Kip hadn't asked her out again on another date weeks after Valentine's Day, which was driving Emma bananas. She couldn't have just imagined their connection that day, right? It was there, bright as daylight, that he was interested in her. Had he changed his mind then? Had she given such a bad literary reference that she'd turned him off completely? Was he just being nice that day? Because she would rather stab herself with a spork than accept pity for a breakup she'd decided on her own.

'Romance employs a transmuted version of the monomyth structure in which the love interest takes on the role of the antagonist—in that the love interest's goals counters the main character's goals, which should explain why they can't be together,' Emma said.

'In that case,' Kip added. 'The road of trials would be where their compatibility is tested, sort of like a litmus test for what they might be like if they did start a relationship with each other even with diametrically opposing goals. This arc of the story should be able to show that the characters have or will have the skills, persistence, qualities, and virtues they need to survive the trials. And if they do survive, they would have gained experience or tools that will help them in overcoming future obstacles far more complicated and difficult. Think of it as the hero learning to ride a bike with training wheels first before riding the big bikes . . . '

Janey and the rest of their five-member team stared at Kip huddling with them in a circle. They were wearing jerseys in their publishing house's company colours with the logo of a book emblazoned on the front and their names sewn into the back. He stopped talking when he realized that he had more than Emma's attention.

'Enough of that, Alegre. We need a plan,' Janey said, holding out a map of the obstacle course on a clipboard in the middle of their huddle. She looked over her shoulder at the other teams from the other corporate divisions of the company, probably to gauge their team's chances of winning, considering who HR had been able to wrangle for this event. 'Airlines and the head office look like they mean business.'

Emma had asked for the easier events like the breakout room where she didn't have to do much but think and solve puzzles. Janey had somehow convinced her to sign up for the obstacle course instead, bragging to the entire office that she did circuit training with Janey on the regular in the past three months—which was not true. She only went when Janey promised to buy her a bag of MILKY WAY.

'You know I'm a book nerd, right, Janey?' Emma whispered to Janey when the HR manager, Tita Beth, had gone (more like limped) to their desk to force them to choose an event a couple of weeks ago.

'You're young, healthy, and fit—' Janey began, forcing Tita Beth's' signup sheet and waiver on Emma. 'Well, fitter than most people in the office anyway.

Tita grinned sheepishly when Emma only started at the sheet. 'If we can't get five people to volunteer, I'll be forced to play.' She pointed at her knee still wrapped in a cast.

So, sighing, Emma wrote her name on the signup sheet, read the lineup, and saw that she would only be the fourth person to sign up after Janey and a couple of people, a lanky, middle-aged man from logistics and a brawny, Gen Z kid from sales whose suits looked like they were always about to pop a button every time he flexed his chest. 'You're short one person, Tita.'

'I'll sign up,' Kip said out of the blue and without looking up from the document he was editing, which was a surprise because Kip almost never participated in company activities unless it involved booze. Tita Beth squealed and brought her signup sheet to him.

'I'm not even sure I'd get all the way to the end, Janey,' Emma said, stealing glances at Kip working at the other end of their shared table.

The din of conversation among her teammates pulled Emma back to the present, to the talk of delivery routes, of printing schedules, of warehouse space—of literally anything else except how their team could possibly finish this course, let alone win. Even Janey had given up forcing the team to make a plan and was swept into the more comfortable talk of work.

The obstacle course was designed to 'encourage teamwork, foster cooperation, and promote synergy' (whatever that meant), the announcers explained over and over, their voices warping through their megaphones.

One of these days, Emma was going to have Janey explain what the heck synergy was and why the heck it was so important to these corporate bigwigs.

Her gaze swept over the tents at the sidelines of the obstacle course where top brass management had congregated to watch the game. Brent was sidling up to the CEO of their corporate overlords, laughing and pointing at his team in the game. Emma imagined that they were laughing at the word synergy (because it was such a silly word) and not, in fact, at the team the publishing house had managed to scramble up from their very small pool of employees—many of whom would not last through this obstacle course.

Heck, even Emma wasn't sure she'd last, and she was pretty healthy for someone who needed to be forced to exercise by her best friend and who considered a MILKY WAY to be well-rounded meal.

Looking at the obstacle course, Emma could tell that it wasn't designed for the faint of heart and weak of body. In fact, it reminded her of the circuit training and high intensity F45 workouts that Janey had somehow talked her into participating in with her. The difference was, instead of doing each course alone (as is the case for circuit training) or in pairs (like F45), team members had to do each obstacle in threes, and every member had to cross three obstacles consecutively before they could pass to the next person.

The Corporate Organizational Communications Team (COCT) said that the theme of threes was fitting for the company's thirtieth anniversary, which really didn't explain to Emma why they had to suffer for it but seeing the head office team that consisted of ultra-buff athletes, she couldn't help but think that maybe the obstacle course was designed to be difficult on purpose. No doubt to weed out the weaklings, which Emma was more than happy to admit until . . .

'There will be cash prizes for the first, second, and third placers of this event to add to the yearly Christmas party fund and individual cash prizes for the participants of the first-place team,' the announcer blared through the speakers.

With renewed determination, she looked at the obstacle course again and really studied it. She had encountered some form of each obstacle before with Janey: tyre flip, monkey bar relay, mud crawl, inclined wall climbing, and running relay over tyre wheels and then hurdles. There were only five obstacle courses, but the challenge was maintaining stamina throughout three rigorous, consecutive, extended exercises and beating out every other team at every course.

Everywhere, employees from different companies under the umbrella conglomerate cheered for their teams and waved flags in the colours of their brands.

Brent appeared, as if from nowhere, huffing and puffing while he explained to the team that there was more at stake here than a swankier Christmas party. He must have run here from the management tents while Emma had been lost in her thoughts again. Brent said that if they made a good impression here, Corporate might *overlook* their financial status and see them for the small scrappy publishing house that they were. It was followed by a string of unhelpful comments and suggestions on how the team could win the game, which Janey dismissed before sending their boss on his way, saying 'Let the pros handle this, old man.' Only Janey could get away with calling their boss names.

When Brent was gone, Janey called all their attention back to their huddle, looking like she'd seen a ghost. 'All right, team, how are we going to win this?' She smiled expectantly at each of them as if waiting for an easy answer to a physics question. 'Better question, how are we going to survive this?'

'Is it even worth putting up a fight?' Kip asked out of the blue, making Janey glare at him. 'I mean look at our competition.'

Emma and Kip exchanged glances. He really wanted to give up and let the game happen as it happened, but she smirked at him, trying to hide just how nervous she was from him and the team. She had a feeling her faked confidence wasn't translating well on her face based on the way Kip tilted his head while he looked at her questioningly.

She could definitely use the prize money they stood to earn should they win the game, especially if she were to lose her job next year. And they could use the Christmas party fund, either to celebrate getting another year of operations or to go out with a bang.

When no one answered, Janey shrugged and said, 'Let's draw lots on who should do which obstacle—'

'No,' Kip said, invoking his Work-Kip voice that made everyone stand at attention. 'Flores, you're lightest on your feet, you should take the first and last legs of the course,' Kip said, switching glances between Emma and the obstacle course map.

Every obstacle—tyre flip (the tyre in question being as tall as Janey), monkey bar relay, mud crawl, inclined wall climbing, and running relay—had to be done in threes and every member of the team must have at least three consecutive turns at the course. Kip took stock of everyone's strengths and weaknesses and assigned each of them to where they could be more useful—with specialties like speed, flexibility, strength, agility, endurance, etc.

When he was done talking, he looked at each and every one of their astonished faces, pausing at Emma with a heart-stopping look on his face that made her thirsty. 'If Corporate wants to shut us down, then we'll show them that we're not going down without a fight.' He brought in a hand and called out, 'Right, team?'

'Right!' Emma's hand shot out over Kip's hand, her palm pressing the hard knuckles of his hand, his fingers. She was tempted to close her palm around his and stopped only when the rest of the team joined them.

'Go, Team Maya! Woohoo!' Janey cheered, hyping them up, and the rest followed.

***

Emma watched Kip in awe (and shameless hunger) as his turn at the course came at the mud crawl, his arms bulging and flexing, the wet mud making his shirt stick to his torso and butt as he crawled over the ground and under a net.

She'd never seen him this way before. He was supposed to be the nerd, hunched over books and manuscripts, hiding

behind thick glasses and under piles of book samples and
proofs, rambling about the nerdiest, most obscure literary
references. If this Kip was a fantasy character, he'd be the
monomyth he'd been rambling about earlier. If this Kip was
a romance novel character, he'd be the alpha billionaire. This
Kip played to win.

Heck, even his grunts amid the noise of the cheering crowd
made the warm well in the pit of her stomach boil, and when
he ran to join her at the inclined wall and grabbed one of the
ropes she held for him and Xander, dragging mud over her
hands, she barely took stock of what she was supposed to do,
which was scale the wall with them.

Xander went up first, and Kip had to wave Emma back
to reality before she could climb the wall after them both.
Xander was the first to reach the ground on the other side of
the inclined wall, thereby finishing his third obstacle course.
He ran to the finish line to wait for the rest of them to finish
their turns.

Kip landed right after, looking up to check on Emma still
at the top of the wall, frozen in place, staring down at the
steep drop, her legs like jelly. There was an earnestness in the
way he looked at her, like he wanted her to take her time, and
she didn't know how it happened, but her hold on the ropes
slipped from the wet mud and she was dropping fast to the
ground. The last thing she saw was Kip's earnest face turning
into a confused then terrified frown before closing her eyes to
wait for impact.

'Emma!' Kip caught her, his body the solid wall breaking
her fall, his arms wrapping around her as they stumbled to
the ground.

When she opened her eyes again, her head was on his chest and he was raising her body as he sat up, frantically checking her head, her arms, her body, for injuries. He cupped her face in his palms, 'Are you okay, Emma? Are you hurt? Talk to me, Emma.'

Time stood still as they stared into each other's eyes, the sounds of the world drowned out by the wild beating of her heart in her chest, in her wrist, in her ears. For a moment, she thought she saw his eyes go down to her lips, parting and pressing closed slowly as cold air passed in and out of her.

Suddenly, like a record screeching to a stop, a rewinding video replayed, the world sped up again, and people began dropping on either side of them, along the wall.

Janey waved her arms at them to call their attention. Kip looked around and pulled them both up.

'Do you want to stop?' he said in his Work-Kip voice, and the power in that tone charged her with a fury and lust that pushed her forward.

She merely shook her head, and he took her hand in his, running forward, making her match his pace, shooting past competitors in a flurry of corporate colours and branding.

Janey was yelling a string of curses at them as they began the cardio and agility part of the course. Janey crossed the finish line first. The whole time, Kip stayed as close as possible to Emma, checking on her, helping her over hurdles, and taking her hand as they ran the last stretch, effectively slowing him down, markedly increasing Emma's speed, so that they ran ahead of most people. They crossed the finish line together, Kip catching her in an embrace as their running slowed down, spinning around, laughing, and holding each like they'd never done before, like they were in a rom-com movie.

It was only when Janey cleared her throat, reminding them that she had run that last leg with them, that they parted, rather reluctantly.

In the end, their team won second place, and the company was given some money to add to their year-end Christmas/going-out-of-business party fund. There were no cash bonuses for second placers, but Emma felt like she'd won the whole race.

Chapter 13

Abstraction

When an author needed to explain a complex, abstract idea within a story in a way that was not forgettable, preachy, or ignorable, they had to write it with a scene that grounded it back to the in-story setting. There was a scale in writing. On one end was abstraction and on the other was concreteness. Brandon Sanderson called this scale the 'Pyramid of Abstraction'. The more abstract the concept, the more it had to be pulled down for clarity. He used the concept of love to explain it, because love meant different things to different people.

Kip taught her that. Apparently, he had watched all of Sanderson's YouTube lectures enough times that he could recite the talk from memory. The thought of his mouth made the insides of her stomach twist into knots, the water tracing lines down her body colder, sharper, more insistent on its impact on her naked skin in the shower.

She hadn't stopped thinking about him since the obstacle course earlier that day, trying to understand what it was that she felt about him now. She decided as the mud washed off her in the shower and swirled down the drain—mud that passed on from his body to hers when he'd caught her, touched her, held her, spun her around—she decided that what she felt was an abstract concept for sure, but what? Was it lust? Was it infatuation? Was it attraction? Was it so abstract that it was love? Or worse, was it all of it? It couldn't be love, right? It was too soon. Too much like a romance story.

'Emma, your phone's ringing,' Janey called from the door of the bathroom. Janey had been too tired to drive back to her house after the company event and had invited herself into staying the night at Emma's place, which she did often anyway after big events like the book fair. 'And I opened the online-store package the courier left at your door. It's underwear!'

'Answer it for me? I'm almost done,' Emma yelled back.

'I don't want to!' Janey said. 'And I don't think you'd want to either. It's Nick.'

Now, that was just as grounding as any other thought. She turned off the shower, wrapped a towel around her body, and came out of her bathroom dripping water on the kitchen floor.

Her cats, who had been waiting for her outside the door, hissed at her and ran back to their cushion under her work-table.

Janey was lounging on the bed, scrolling through social media on her phone, Emma's own phone lighting up with call notifications on the bedside table.

Janey looked up at her with judging eyes.

'Don't look at me like that, Janey,' Emma said, picking up her phone. 'I've met the guys you've dated.'

'None of them were real relationships. And all of them knew without a doubt that it was over between us months after I broke up with them.'

Emma sat on the bed, eyes on Nick's name on the screen, her shoulders sinking. He was going to ask her out on a *friendly* dinner date again. 'Don't you ever want to, you know . . . be in a real, without a doubt, relationship?'

That made Janey put down her phone. 'Why would I? I'm fine on my own.'

'Don't you ever get . . . '

'Get what?'

'Scared.'

'Of what?'

'Being alone.'

Janey paused, looking at Emma as if unsure if that answer had really come from her. 'What's this really about, Emma? Why are you turning this on me?'

'It's just . . . I don't think I've ever been on my own, my entire life until now. I've always had my mother. Now she's gone. I'd been in a relationship with Nick for six years. Now we're broken up. I don't know how to be . . . alone, I guess.'

'So, you keep Nick around just in case it gets too scary?'

'Sometimes, I can't help but think that I made the wrong decision, Janey. Aren't we supposed to fight for love when times get hard, to keep choosing love even after the infatuation or the affection or the lust is gone. Love is continuing to choose each other even if the feeling isn't there any more, isn't it?'

Janey propped herself up on her elbows and levelled Emma with a piercing, questioning gaze. 'Don't you see the problem there?'

'What problem?'

'It's not love if you don't love him. Infatuation, affection, and lust are not the same as love.'

'But I do care for him still.'

'Is that enough? You don't love Nick in the way he needs you to love him. Not any more.'

'How are you so sure it's not love any more?'

Janey shrugged. 'Easy. If there's doubt, even a shadow of it, in how you feel, it's not love. It's a murky, abstract copy of the feeling, but not *the* feeling.'

'How would you know if it *is* love?'

Janey shrugged again. 'I don't think I've ever been in love that way before. I imagine I would just know, and I'd do everything and anything to take it for myself.'

Emma's fingers hovered over the keyboard in the chat bar of her conversation with Nick.

'Don't do it, Emma,' Janey said, scrolling through her phone again. 'It's not fair to you or Nick . . . or Kip.'

Emma held back a gasp. 'Kip? What does he have to do with this?'

This time, Janey sat up and stared at her, studying her face, looking for the lie or the pretence, none of which she found.

'You don't see it, do you?' she said.

'What don't I see?' Emma asked, moving to grab Janey by the shoulders to make her answer, but Janey, fitter, stronger, more agile than her, evaded her as she picked up an opened courier box on the floor and plopped it on the bed.

'It's not my secret to tell,' Janey said. 'But maybe you should get better underwear. You know, just in case.'

Emma put her phone down on the table, Nick's message forgotten, grabbed the box from Janey, and pulled out bras and panties printed with cats from literature and cats dressed as literary characters. 'They're cute. What's wrong with these?'

'What's not?'

'They make me laugh.'

'You won't be the only one laughing.'

'It's not like anyone will ever see them. Well, anyone but you.'

'You wanna bet?' Janey said, flicking her brows up and down like she was in on a plan that Emma wasn't sure she understood.

Chapter 14

Follies and Nonsense

In publishing, the deadline was king unless the printing machine didn't have the capacity to produce the entire print run before the target release date. Everyone else—editorial, production, circulations, publishers—had to fall in line for it.

Which was why Kip went to the factory to oversee his book projects being printed. His books for the Summer Komikon in April were cutting it really close. They had Kip living in the dormitory quarters of the factory over the weekend, to save time on deliveries and check signature proofs—the template by which production managers based the actual products coming out of the machines.

Because Amora had sent in the newest revised draft of *Menagerie* last week and they'd both sworn that they'd talk about their edits after a week, Emma decided it made sense that she went with him.

'Are you sure you want to go? It means you'll have to work on a weekend,' Kip said reluctantly as she got into the front passenger seat of his car on the Saturday morning that he picked her up at her condo.

If she was being honest with herself, it wasn't such a bad thing having to work over the weekend if it meant she could be with Kip. To work on *Menagerie*, mostly, but she wouldn't mind just seeing more of him if she could help it.

The factory manager hadn't expected two people to come so they had only prepared the men's quarters. Before Kip could say anything, like suggesting that he drive her back to her condo, she answered for him, saying that she'd be okay sleeping in the same room with Kip if it was all right with everybody.

'It's not like we have to share a bed, right?' she joked.

'Nothing like the romance trope,' Kip answered, bringing up the time she'd taught him the most popular romance tropes.

They had the spartan dormitory all to themselves, but they each got a bed across from the other's, closer to the door—and therefore the shared bathroom. While Kip went to watch the printing machines work, Emma mostly stayed in their room. At first, she kept up the pretence of working, so that whenever Kip returned between signature proofs, he would catch her working. She didn't actually need to. The next bulk of work for her assigned genres would be for the September book fair anyway, and she had already read the newest draft of *Menagerie* and compiled her comments in their shared online document for this project.

By Kip's third break for lunch, she had given up, laid on the bed on her stomach, facing away from the door, and played *Pride And Prejudice* on her laptop.

Midway through the movie, just as Ann de Bourgh was finally being introduced, a whisper to her ear sent titillating chills on the back of her neck, 'Slacking off on our social duties, aren't we, Ms Bennet?'

She pressed pause on the movie and looked over her shoulder at him, an idea coming to her, follies and nonsense indeed.

'Follies and nonsense, whims and inconsistencies,' Emma began, issuing a challenge. *'—do divert me, I own, and I laugh at them whenever I can.'*

She saw the corner of his lips rise in a pleased but hesitant smile and felt her bed dipping under his weight, his right knee pressing up against her side. '*Nothing is more deceitful* . . . ' he answered, another breathy whisper into her ear, an acceptance of the game. ' . . . *than the appearance of humility. It is often only carelessness of opinion, and sometimes an indirect boast.*'

She felt him leaning into her, his body so close she could feel his heat on her back. She was losing breath when she spoke again, her racing heart making just the act of talking difficult. '*There is, I believe, in every disposition a tendency to some particular evil—a natural defect, which not even the best education can overcome.*'

Thank god she had just watched the movie. Her mind was barely functioning now, let alone remembering long-winded Jane Austen quotes.

He inhaled a sharp, unsteady breath, his answer the shot to the heart, the last nail on the coffin, '*You showed me how insufficient were all my pretensions to please a woman worthy of being pleased.*'

That made her turn over sharply, dragging Kip with her and forcing him to fall on top of her, pressing all of his weight on her body and pinning her to the bed, their faces so close that if she nudged slightly, her lips would find his too easily.

She didn't dare move, not even breathe normally, because the exhale of her breath against his cheek would turn her insides into hot molten lava raging along the rivers of her already overheating body.

She didn't need to do anything, because he leaned into her, capturing her mouth in his with a chaste, reluctant, fearful kiss. He pulled away before they went any deeper and went to his bed, their bodies parting as palpable as ripping paper in two.

Face pale, as if in shock, he sat on his bed and opened his phone mechanically. 'What do you want for lunch, Buttercup?'

he asked shakily, pretending and failing to act as if he hadn't just kissed her, leaving her blinking with confusion on her bed.

She sat up sharply and glared at him. 'What was that?'

'What was what?' he asked without looking up from his phone, face flushed. 'You want Jollibee? Or are you craving something fancier?'

'Kip,' she said sternly. 'Why did you stop? Better yet, why haven't you asked me out on another date? Just why?'

Kip sighed and put down his phone. 'I'm afraid.'

'Of?' She folded her arms over her chest. 'Jane Austen?'

He didn't answer for a long while, looking at her as if hoping he could articulate to her what he really wanted to say with his eyes, which were begging her not to make him answer. She doubled down on her glare until one word from what could be a very long explanation just slipped out. 'You.'

'You're going to have to be more forthright than that.'

'Look. My last breakup was devastating, and I don't . . . I don't think I can handle it again . . . '

She arched an eyebrow at him, urging him to continue, but to do it cautiously.

' . . . If it were you who broke my heart.' He averted his gaze when he said that.

Her arms dropped to her sides slowly, surprised by the honesty and sincerity of it. Without thinking, she went to him and wrapped her arms around his shoulder, letting him burrow his face into her chest. He didn't do anything at first, just sat there, stiff and afraid and confused and surprised, but eventually, his hands found her waist and slid to the small of her back, pressing her against him.

She nuzzled her face in his hair, the scent of ink, paper, sweat, and his natural musk filling her with so much need and urgency, like if he didn't give her a straight answer now, she'd just spontaneously combust in his arms. 'How will you know that I won't break your heart if you don't give me a chance?' she said. 'We can take it slowly if you want.'

He took his time answering, and after a few minutes of just letting him hold her, of just holding him back, he nodded. That was answer enough for now.

Chapter 15

Clichés and Overused Tropes

Emma hadn't been making good choices this past week.

She'd promised another book production timeline that she couldn't possibly meet if she wanted any work-life balance. Again. She'd tried giving a new brand of cat food to her cats, and they hated it—and thus, they hated her. She was afraid of what she'd find in her unit when she got home. She'd promised Janey she'd try a new version of F45 with her next, which, if the advertisement were to be believed, would only be a modified, abridged version of circuit training. She didn't believe it.

But this, going to the Summer Komikon, the biggest and nerdiest comic book convention in the country, even when she didn't have to, she didn't regret this choice. Because Kip was here.

She'd come with the excuse of wanting to borrow the latest book in *The Stormlight Archive*—a hardbound thousand-plus-page SFF monstrosity that she could barely carry with both her arms—which she was reading laid out on the table of their company's booth, in the area where their authors sat for book signings. Janey was hovering around the booth during and between signings and going off to talk to event organizers every so often, while one rep each from circulations and accounting alternated shifts, manning the cash register and replenishing inventory. This was one of those events where editors were better off staying out of the way, which Emma and Kip were not at all inclined to do. Kip was passionate about his book projects, and it always filled him with such joy just seeing the books he had been working on for months finally being sold.

Emma had been stealing glances at Kip as he sold books, explained every book's premise, and made comparisons with other titles. That sparkle in his eye that came and went when he figured out an edit or when he found a gem of a story from the slush pile stayed on his face the entire day. He stole glances at her every so often, and he'd smile when he met her eyes. He was like a light bulb that sparked with so much energy, and she felt like a moth to the flame, *gamo-gamo* to the light before the rain. It didn't matter that the book she was reading could be the greatest and most ambitious SFF story of their generation. Kip was the monomyth incarnate.

When people dwindled during the lunch rush, he sat next to her, drinking water, and stealing glances at the page she was on. She was mesmerized by his Adam's apple bobbing up and down his throat, suddenly feeling so very thirsty herself.

'I know you're a slow reader, but you're not even past the prologue, Buttercup,' he said, flipping through the pages of the book in front of her.

She swallowed the lump in her throat, her mind blanking while she desperately scrounged for an excuse. He was looking at her so earnestly, and she didn't want to sound like an idiot. 'Well . . . ' She cleared her throat, hoping to buy herself time. 'Sorry, Hobbit. I didn't know I was on a deadline.'

'You're not. You can borrow the book for as long as you want,' he said, a hand going to that spot on her nape, his thumb stroking her skin fondly. 'Sanderson experiments with classic SFF tropes and puts them in the context of today's most relevant issues like mental health, gender equality, as well as colonial mentality. In *Mistborn*, he twisted the chosen one–dark lord dynamic so that the chosen one brought the demise of the world and not its salvation.'

'That's the trend now in SFF stories, isn't it? Taking a widely used trope and turning it around its head so it's barely recognizable on the page,' Emma said. 'Nobody wants classic SFF any more.'

'But that's the magic, I think, of SFF. You never know what you get. Someone's always experimenting. Even *The Lord of The Rings* took the chosen one trope, something so overused in the fantasies of that time, and made Frodo choose his destiny for himself. The chosen one books of late twist it further by making the chosen one the dark lord like *Dune*, *Red Rising*, and even *The Poppy War*.'

'Is this another crash course into SFF?' she said, narrowing her eyes at him.

'I guess now is a good time for it,' he said, pressing his fingers to his chin to feign some deep consideration and then smirking when he saw the impatient look on her face.

'So, tell me how are you going to relate this to *Menagerie*, which is essentially a romance to the core?'

'Just because many SFF books are about war, politics, and the apocalypse doesn't mean there aren't love stories in there. In fact, love is the underlying theme of many of these books. Let's go back to Grandpa Tolkien, and the love story that had such a major impact, though not directly, on the events of the trilogy. Beren and Luthien, Arwen and Aragorn's ancestors—'

He stopped abruptly to face Janey who was glaring at him with her hands on her hips. 'You two are taking up space. I've got authors coming for the afternoon signings.'

'All right, all right, I'm leaving,' he said, standing and gathering his things. Emma did the same and grinned at Janey, who was making eyes at her that asked, 'What is going on here?'

After Kip hefted his backpack on one shoulder, he picked up the heavy book that Emma was reading and offered a hand to her. 'Lunch, Buttercup?'

She met Janey's eyes, which were wide as saucers, and shrugged when Janey mouthed, 'Buttercup?'

Emma took Kip's offered hand, and he intertwined their fingers. 'See you later, Flores,' he said.

Emma mouthed, 'Sorry! I'll text you!' before she left with Kip.

***

Emma turned their entire afternoon together into the most nerve-racking and least rewarding game of chicken—thanks to Janey, who had all but flooded her inbox with some version of 'Explain yourself!' Why did she suddenly feel self-conscious and hyper aware of Kip's constant proximity to her body?

He'd sit next to her, eating ice cream nonchalantly, close enough that his thigh pressed against hers, and he'd talk about some other world, as if this world they were creating right here, this new galaxy of her and him, was fiction and the stories were real-life.

'Arwen and Aragorn's relationship is not even mentioned in the main text, but their story goes way back to their ancestor Beren and Luthien, whom Aragorn thought he saw when he first saw Arwen . . . '

She hung on to his every word, pushed right at the edge of her seat hoping this moment didn't stop. It seemed he didn't want it to stop too, and his stories snowballed further and further into the deepest trenches of genre fiction.

When the last lick of ice cream was gone, he took her on a walking tour of the books that he loved. It was just a bookstore nearby, but to him, it held a thousand universes, a million worlds, billions of lives. His palm fell on the small of her back, on the curve of her shoulder, on the back of her arm as he ushered her from one world to another.

'Arrakis is an ecological study of life on worlds without water . . . '

As they walked between shelves in the SFF section, he'd pick out book after book, easing her into his world like a pilgrim finding a place to settle down.

'*Outlander* began as a romance story, but the author ultimately intended to expand the love story from a handsome Scotsman falling in love with a modern English woman to a lifetime built in love from the meet-cute till death do us part. Plus, time travel.'

He hovered close to her, looking over her shoulder to check out the page she was reading, so close she felt his breath on her cheek—chocolate-mint-ice-cream scented. She was suddenly very aware that her mouth still tasted like strawberries and cream.

'The Highstorms of Roshar dictate how life survives on its planet. So, the inhabitants of the planet grow hard shells on their bodies and build homes that can withstand constantly destructive weather . . . '

When he reached for a book on the shelf in front of her, his body behind her felt like a storm mercilessly delaying landfall, till the thunderstorm raged inside her, bubbling in the pit of her stomach and boiling over in her chest and between her thighs.

'A lot of classic genre fiction follows the hero's journey or the monomyth archetype. It's not essentially about a chosen one defeating evil-incarnate, though that is the end goal of these plot lines, but more about the growth of the chosen-one character from say dumb kid living on a moisture farm in the middle of nowhere to the greatest Jedi in the galaxy.'

Trembling, she turned to him, only the open book spread across her chest blocking her from him, her phone in her other hand. Breathing felt like a chore.

His jaw clenched, hesitation flashing in the back of his eyes again, followed by an epiphany and a reluctance to act on it. He looked into her eyes, question after question asked wordlessly—'Is this okay?', 'Are we going too fast?', 'Is this going too slow?', 'Do you want me as much as I want you?'

When he pulled back, that was when she knew she'd lost the game. She impulsively pulled at the hem of his clothes, looking up at his face, his body towering over her, shelves filled to the brim with books, a thousand stories flanking them like sentinels.

He smiled at her, patient, curious, hopeful, and then leaned in just enough to close the gap . . .

Her phone rang, and he pulled away, breaking apart the galaxy before the big bang, his eyes on the screen of her phone, on the name that had once made her stomach flutter but now made it churn.

'You should answer that, Emma,' he said, a bleak expression that she had never seen on him falling on his smiling face, before walking away. She let the ringing die a natural death while she watched Kip traverse a different row of shelves, creating a wall between them, another galaxy apart.

Nick's message came after. 'Will you come to my next gig? I want to know what you think of my new song.'

Chapter 16

Believable Dialogue

'Start talking,' Janey said, stepping on the treadmill right next to Emma's. They met the day after the second day of Komikon to work out at the gym. 'And your explanation better be good.'

She'd talked Janey out of doing circuit training—'Janey, you just pulled off a two-day book signing event,' Emma replied 'You shouldn't force yourself to do high intensity interval training right after.'

So here they were, in sports bras and yoga pants, running at the same speed on their respective machines, Emma just trying to catch her breath and Janey looking like she was taking a leisurely walk at the park. The gym was packed tonight. Most machines and equipment were in use. Brawny men huddled up close to the weights, watching themselves in the mirror as they did sets with barbells, dumbbells, and kettlebells. The women, many of whom were wearing headphones, were gathered in another corner of the room, close to the yoga room and the cardio machines. Somehow two treadmill machines were conveniently made available for Janey thanks to the coach she had been making eyes with since they'd got here.

'I don't think I can even talk,' Emma said between pants as she tried and failed to keep up with Janey. 'Can we do it *after* we get off the treadmill?'

Janey let out a big exhale and decreased the speed of both their machines so that they were just speed walking. Emma was still panting, but she could talk, albeit breathily.

'It just happened,' Emma said, wanting to give as short an explanation as she could to save breath. 'He asked me out on Valentine's Day—'

'Valentine's Day! And you waited this long to tell me?'

'He didn't ask me out again for months after. It wasn't worth talking about!'

'Typical Kip, giving up without putting up a real fight.'

'What does *that* mean?'

'Kip never plays unless he knows for sure he'll win. Remember the company sports fest? He *wanted* to give up.'

'He did seem like it at first, but he didn't.'

'We all thought he had a concussion when he suddenly took charge,' Janey said, walking briskly, her platinum blonde hair swinging wildly behind her. 'But now that I think about it, he probably had a different prize in mind.' She arched an eyebrow at Emma questioningly. 'So, something must have happened since Valentine's Day that scared him away.'

Janey was right, and Kip did say he was scared she'd break his heart back at the factory. But she wasn't going to tell Janey about that, about what happened there. That moment was too surreal, too intimate to want to share outside of her and Kip's galaxy.

'Does he know about Nick?' Janey asked out of the blue, pulling Emma out of that intimate memory.

'What does Nick have to do with this?'

'You have history with Nick, and no matter how much you deny it, he's still holding out hope that you'd take him back, you know.'

'That can't be it. He knows for sure that the most I could give him is friendship. I tell him that over and over again when we go out.'

Janey's brows shot upward so fast, Emma thought she heard the whiplash. 'You . . . go out . . . with Nick?'

'Yeah. For dinner and coffee.' Emma thought about her answer, thinking that it wasn't clear enough, so she added, 'Not dates.'

'Oh, Emma. Emma, Emma, Emma.'

'What?'

'You naïve, oblivious, cruel little bitch.'

Emma scowled. 'You better explain that, or I'm going to take that as a real insult.'

'No wonder Nick is still holding out hope,' Janey said. 'And Kip is reluctant to go all the way with you.'

Emma turned off her machine to face Janey fully so she could speak without trying to catch her breath. 'That implies that I'm stringing two men along, Janey. I'm not. Nick and I are over, and I want something more with Kip. The issue is with them and not me.'

'True,' Janey agreed, not stopping her treadmill. 'It's not your fault, but you did say that you were afraid to be alone.'

Emma levelled her with a serious, warning look.

'Okay, okay, I'll stop—' Janey stopped her machine, '—if you say that you know for sure that you're not relieved that Nick is still there in case things with Kip don't pan out.'

Emma's jaw dropped, her lips parting to say words that she didn't know were true, but nothing came out. 'Of course, I'm not relieved!' Emma was forced to say, seeing that Janey's expression was changing into one that said she was sorry for being right about this.

'Good,' Janey answered. 'You can't do anything about Nick now, except press upon him that it is indeed over between you. And you need to assure Kip that you won't break his heart.'

'What if I introduce Kip to Nick? I'm going to one of his gigs soon. I could bring Kip there.'

'Everything about that plan screams "bad idea."'

'Well, what do you want me to do? Force Kip to sleep with me?'

'You don't have to force him,' Janey said, starting their machines again. 'Something tells me that Kip is only waiting for your consent—and opportunity.' Her brows went up and down knowingly at Emma. 'Maybe he'll like your literature cats underwear. He's nerdy enough to get it.'

***

Janey decided that thirty minutes on the treadmill hadn't been enough for her and decided to join a circuit training class after all. Emma begged off the class, promising that she'd do weights instead.

As she made her way to the rows of dumbbells, she stopped, a cold shiver running down her spine and a hot pang boiling in the pit of her stomach and her thighs.

Kip was standing in front of a mirror in a black skin-tight Under Armour shirt, loose black pants, white rubber shoes, and his usual thick black-rimmed glasses, hair wet with sweat, body tense and coiled tight like rope, arms flexing under the weight of two thirty-five-pound dumbbells, grunting like a feral animal with every lift.

Her mind went blank, the words *Hot nerd! Hot nerd! Hot nerd!* shamelessly screaming like sirens in the empty space.

It was as if her body had grown a mind of its own and was fighting with her own mind, so she just stood there frozen in indecision. Her stomach churned. Her skin turned hot and cold at the same time. She wanted to run the tips of her tingling fingers over his arms, his chest, his shoulders, his neck, his face.

His face was a picture of extreme concentration as he hefted the dumbbells up in a bicep curl, watching himself in the mirror as he did. Finishing that set, he put the pair of dumbbells down, and went for a heavier one to use for an overhead tricep extension, which showed off the shape of his torso as his arms raised upward. Who knew he had all that hiding under his nerd shirts? And he hasn't even taken off his shirt.

She must have been standing there behind him for an awkwardly long time because his eyes darted to her as he counted. He stopped his set, recognition in his eyes, and lowered the dumbbell slowly to the floor. 'Emma?'

Suddenly, all of Emma's wits returned to her head in one swift blow that felt like a punch to the face, kicking in her fight or flight instinct. She had no words to say so she fled, running back to the women's locker room to hide until Janey finished her class.

When she did, a little over half an hour later, Janey said, 'Kip says hi, and that he'll see you at the office.' And that was the end of that.

That night, she dreamt of Kip on her bed, his large mass climbing on top of her. There wasn't much sleeping done that night, or dreaming, or talking for that matter. There was just doing and the promise of it actually happening when the opportunity arose.

Chapter 17

The Ignition Temperature

Kip joked that if the months of this year were books, July was *Fahrenheit 451*.

They were in publishing. It was book fair season. And paper burns at 451 degree fahrenheit. Emma thought it was hilarious and was still laughing at the joke well past midnight. The rest of the office just groaned. The third quarter of the yearly publishing cycle was usually spent trying to get as many books out as possible before the book fair in September.

They had ten books slated for that month alone, which meant more man hours and longer days for the editorial, art, and production teams. It was about 1.00 a.m. when Jesse and the last graphic artist left for home, leaving Kip and Emma alone in the office, sitting across from each other on the table close to the proofing machine with a pile of proofs and so much sexual tension it could set their office on fire.

No one had brought up what happened at the gym, but neither needed to anyway. They both knew what it meant. They were both only waiting for consent and opportunity, which Emma was more than willing to give. If he asked. Which he didn't.

They worked in relative silence then, listening to each other's breaths, the scratch of pens on glossy proofing paper, and the quiet sounds of an empty office after a long, tiring day. They took comfort in the fact that they weren't alone, and if Emma would allow herself the indulgence, comfort in the fact that they were with each other.

At 2.00 a.m., Kip and Emma looked up from their respective piles at almost exactly the same time, looking so exhausted, haggard, and sleep-deprived that they couldn't help laughing at each other, startling the guard who was doing his rounds on the floor.

Emma had taken off her contacts in favour of her big round dorky glasses and tied her hair up in a messy bun on top of her head. Kip's own hair was a big mop of curls that had a just-woke-up-from-bed look.

'Alone in the trenches again, Buttercup,' Kip said, taking off his glasses and pinching the bridge of his nose. 'Can't say I missed this part of the job from the pre-pandemic days.'

Emma put down her own pen and slumped into her chair. 'Honestly, I'm just glad we're making books again.'

'You thought we'd never make books again after the pandemic years, didn't you?'

'Did you?' she asked in a pitch higher than she intended.

'I couldn't have known then. All I knew was that I could never imagine doing anything else other than making books.'

'Have you thought about it? What'll happen to us when—if the company folds? What are you going to do?'

He looked up at the ceiling, taking his time to answer as if he had never given it much thought until she asked now. 'I might join my family in New Zealand.'

He kept his face tilted up, but his eyes looked at her from across the table, a knowing smile sliding on his lips. A toothy, teasing grin grew on Emma's face, and she caught the quirk in the corner of his lips. 'Just come out with it, Buttercup.'

'New Zealand? Like Hobbiton? Does your family live in a real-life Hobbit hole? Are you an actual Hobbit, Kip?'

'Ha-ha! Sorry to disappoint you, but it's just a two-storey red brick house with big windows.'

'Boo! Such a buzzkill, Hobbit,' she said then laughed at the bemused yet resigned expression on Kip's face.

'That's it, Buttercup. Get it out of your system,' Kip said, picking up his pile of proofs, taking them back to the proofing machine, and putting them on the shelf assigned to a printer.

Emma followed suit, placing her own pile on another printer's shelf.

'What about you? What will you be doing after?' Kip said, leaning casually on the wall behind the proofing machine, as he watched her sort through her proofs on the shelf.

Emma looked up at the ceiling. These past seven months, she had avoided thinking about what she was going to do if the company folded. Either she went full freelance or corporate communications. Those were her only options given how small the book publishing industry actually was in the Philippines. There was a growing lump in her throat at the thought. Kip was watching her the whole time, waiting for the answer, and she could only shrug. 'I hope I get to still make books. I can't imagine myself doing anything else.'

'Are we suckers for wanting to do a job that's likely not going to make us rich?'

'I don't know,' she said. 'I just know that we'd be even bigger suckers not to do it if the chance is available to us.'

His face sliced into a big smile, like he was a child being handed a ball for the first time after watching the big kids play with it. A warmth bloomed in her chest, exploding outward at the sight of his smile, sincere, genuine, amused, earnest at this ungodly hour. It pleased her that she made him smile like that.

And that moment of quiet epiphany stretched out between them, weaving invisible lines, filling in the white space in the gap that separated their bodies. Without his glasses, she could see his big brown eyes, unadulterated, pure, unencumbered by myopic barriers. She could stare into them all day—had she not let out an ugly, loud, big-mouthed, definitely-not-cute yawn.

He laughed out loud and led the way back to their table. 'Let's call it a night, Emma.'

She nodded, following him, covering her face as she did another ugly yawn. 'Are you driving at this hour?'

'Afraid so, Buttercup.' The jangle of keys in his pocket and the zipping of bags punctuated the end of this long day—one that Emma was, surprisingly, disappointed to see ending.

That's when an idea came to her, a very dumb, impulsive idea, that she was sure he'd think was a weird suggestion coming from her. Consent and opportunity, right? 'Why don't you stay the night?' she blurted out, slapping her forehead in her mind and following him into the lobby in front of the elevator.

His head turned sharply to her, the valley between his brows deepening again like he was unsure he had understood her correctly. 'At your place?' he said, voice two octaves higher.

'I mean, just to wait out the night!' she blurted out again, unsure if she made sense or if she was just rambling. She added more words that sounded dumber and dumber to her ears. 'You live far away. It's not safe driving at this ungodly—'

'Okay!' he said, his head jerking like he was startled by his own answer, then shook his head, laughing. 'Okay,' he said, calmer, more certain this time.

They stood facing each other, her chin tilting upwards to look into his brown eyes, him leaning down to her, trying to fill the space between them. The memory of mint chocolate came to her when his breath touched her cheek. The warmth of his skin created heat lines that melded with her own. It was so quiet that the world was drowned out by her own thundering heart.

The elevator dinged, the doors slid open.

She nodded, swallowing the lump in her throat.

When did it suddenly get so hot here?

Like *Fahrenheit 451* hot?

***

The sound of the shower running in her bathroom made Emma's throat desert-dry, and she took her time staring at the bathroom door in front of the refrigerator, holding a cold glass of water to her neck. Two of her cats were lounging about her unit. Wentworth was staring longingly out the window under her desk, and Knightley was trying to provoke Wentworth into playing with him. Only Darcy was at her feet, sitting on his haunches and quietly judging her with his blue eyes.

'Don't judge me, Darcy. I've seen the cats you tramp with in the communal garden,' she said to Darcy, who looked unfazed. 'He'll just wait out the night. It's not safe to drive at this hour. Highway robbery and all.' Still staring judgingly at her. 'We're just friends, Darcy. Colleagues! I think. I'm not actually sure. Sheesh! Nothing's going to happen.' The cat looked like he rolled his eyes as he shifted his attention from her, squirming uncomfortably where she stood, to the bathroom door, which opened at the exact same time she raised her eyes to look.

Kip made eye contact with her, surprised to see her standing there outside the door.

'Who were you talking to?' he said, drying his overgrown hair with a towel. He wore a white cotton shirt that stuck to his still damp skin, showing off the shape of his body underneath, and blue-grey striped pyjamas pants—clothes that Nick had left here when they were still dating.

'Uhm . . . Darcy,' she said, turning to the refrigerator again to refill her glass.

'Your cat?' he said, bemused, leaning on the kitchen counter next to the refrigerator so he was facing her. 'I think Darcy likes me.'

Emma looked down at the black cat weaving between Kip's legs. 'Traitor,' she mouthed at the cat, who merely hissed back at her before joining his brothers.

'Don't they get lonely staying cooped up here in your unit?'

'I let them out in the communal garden once a week where the other stray cats are. But mostly, they hate going outside, and they punish me when I try to take them out,' she said, pressing the glass to her lips, staring at him over the rim. The towel she'd lent him was draped over his shoulders, his dark brown hair still dripping over it. He'd put his glasses back on again, and he was looking over her shoulder, that valley between his brows deepening. She followed his line of sight and saw her bed there, so imposing and so, so . . . singular. Panic rose like bile to her throat, her heart beating at breakneck speed, her skin turning cold. The realization dawned on her like a sledgehammer to the face.

One bed. There was only one bed.

'There's just one bed,' she said as if saying it out loud would throw it back into fiction where it belonged, and a second bed would appear in its wake like magic.

'I can sleep on the floor, Buttercup,' Kip said, focusing his gaze on her with a concerned, confused look on his face. 'Are you okay?'

She met his eyes again and said, 'Just one bed.' It's the romance gods again and their twisted sense of humour. She burst out laughing, doubling over and clutching at her stomach.

'I don't understand . . . ' he said, more amused by her laughter than the joke.

'There's just one bed. Like the trope!' she said between fits of laughter, spilling a bit of water from the glass clutched tightly in her other hand.

Clarity lit up his face, and finally, he laughed with her, too. They were just two book nerds standing in the middle of a nerdy joke.

When finally, the laugh mellowed into giggles and then quick breaths, their eyes met again, faces flushed and eyes sparkling with pure joy. Finally, the context of the punchline made itself known. One bed and two characters that had manifested sexual tension since the beginning of their story.

He closed the distance between them so that the smell of her soap on his skin sent shivers down her spine. Then, he took the glass of water from her hand and pressed his lips where her own had left an imprint, condensation dripping down the side of the glass and on to his hand, as he drank. She watched his Adam's apple bobbing up and down with every swallow, feeling like time was stretching so unbelievably and annoyingly slowly. Why had she poured so much water into that glass?

Without breaking eye contact with her, he set the empty glass down on the counter and said, 'Hi, Buttercup.'

'Hi, Hobbit,' she answered breathlessly before standing on her tiptoes and pressing her lips on his. Before he could kiss her back, she pulled away, only to be pulled back to him with two hands on her hips. She pressed her palms on his shoulders, and she felt his hand trace a line up her forearm, her clavicle, her neck, and then her jaw, the sweet slow act culminating with a gentle tuck of hair behind her ear. He cupped her cheek in his hand, his brown eyes almost not believing that they were here now, staring at each other through their glasses.

'You're wearing the *Star Wars* shirt again, Buttercup,' he said, a laugh in his voice.

'Oh, sorry.' She looked down, hands attempting to cover her embarrassing ratty sleeping clothes, but he stopped her, shaking his head as he wrapped her arms around his neck.

'No, I like it,' he said, grinning as his hands found purchase around her waist, pressing her to him so that their bodies were aligned, hip to hip, torso to torso, chest to chest. He looked at her face hungrily, tenderly as if memorizing every inch of her now, with her glasses, her hair bunched up in a bun on top of her head, her pink lips slightly parted. 'May I kiss you?'

Her body answered before her words could, and nodding, she leaned up to him, standing on her tiptoes to meet his height, kissing him, and this time allowing him to kiss back.

There was an art to the kiss, two characters learning the feel of the other's lips, their hunger, their wanting, pressed against the other's. There was a spectrum of hunger to it, a gauge by which to judge how much the other had wanted to do this since they'd first met. Starving, partners forget all else, the world falls away, it is just them consuming and taking as much as they can and giving up everything, everything, everything. Chaste, it is two characters playing a game, making a promise, asking question after question after question and at the same time pleading, begging, wanting the other without giving away everything in one all-consuming shared moment and then walking away hungry for more, as if saving every little morsel of hunger for another day. They both fell somewhere in between.

She initiated it. She parted her lips for him and let him in, his teeth nipping at her bottom lip, her tongue dipping into him. Without breaking their kiss, Kip picked her up easily, and gasping, she wrapped her legs around his waist as he carried her further into her home. He pressed her against her bookshelf, his body firmly lodged between her legs, laying her on one shelf so that his face was level with hers against the backdrop of her literature. He was Darcy walking in the rain. He was Simon saying, 'I burn for you.' He was Edward catching her scent for the first time.

He wandered over her body as she explored his. Neck. Ears. Cheek. Clavicle. Hair. Shoulder. Chest. Throat. Lips. They were terraformers on Mars. They were the Iron Rain charging a planet ripe for invasion. They were the Force that bound their separate galaxies together.

Kip's hands slipped under her shirt, and she pulled away from him, looking at him, looking so deep in his eyes that she could not find words. Just one, 'Please,' and she led his hands further up and under her shirt to cup her breasts. 'Please, Kip.'

But she didn't need so many words. He understood immediately what she wanted, knew the context of the story she was writing with his hands on her body.

'Birth control?' he asked with his lips still against her neck.

'Yes,' she said, feeling the vibration of the word on her throat that answered the question on his lips. 'Hurry.'

He nodded, going back to her ears, breathing the word 'Okay' with mint-chocolate breath.

'Do you have any?' she asked, her hands slipping under the waistband of his pants.

He pulled away sharply, staring sheepishly at her, 'You don't have any?'

She shook her head, feeling just as sheepish as he looked. 'I didn't think I'd need them after the breakup.'

'Oh god. I feel like such a dork right now.' He nuzzled his face into the crook of her neck. 'Of all the things for us to have in common, it's this.'

'You mean, not expecting to get any action after our respective breakups?' she said with a laugh.

'Yeah. Besides, what would you think of me if I went to work every day with condoms in my pocket just to see you?'

'Like you know a version of a happy ending that I really, really, really want,' she said, her face in his hair. 'Wait.' Hands on his shoulders, she pushed him away so that she could see his face. 'You go to the office every day just to see me? Hours and hours of driving even on days I don't go?'

He nodded with an embarrassed grin. 'Is that creepy?'

'No,' she said hesitantly at first, then followed it up with 'Not at all' when she decided that it wasn't creepy. Not to her. Sighing, she hopped off the shelf. 'We don't have to do anything, Kip. I didn't bring you here just for that.' She sat on the bed, leaned back into the headboard, and patted the space next to her. 'Well, not just that,' she said with a teasing roll of her eyes. 'Besides, you look like you're half-dead from exhaustion.'

He sat next to her and pulled her body to him, her face resting on his chest. 'Gee. I could say the same to you, Buttercup, but I'd be lying.'

'Why?' she said with a gasp and slapped his arm in jest. 'Because I already look dead?'

'No, because you're beautiful,' he said, planting a kiss on her forehead. 'You're always beautiful.' He tilted her face up with a thumb on her chin. 'Are you sure this is okay? I could do this . . . ' His hand traced his fingers down her body and over her inner thigh.

She kissed him, slower this time, savouring him, then shook her head. 'No, we're both tired from work. I can't do that to you.'

'By all means, Buttercup. I'd work so fucking hard for you.'

She laughed into his chest. 'I'm sure I can find work for you—' She pressed her index finger to his lip. '—another time, Hobbit. Let's just go to sleep. We've still got work tomorrow. Amora sent her revised manuscript today.'

He groaned. 'Jesse's been angling for a promotion. I'm sure she can handle a day without us.'

'Kip!'

'Fine!' he said, wrapping his arms around her body. 'Just so you know, I don't think I'll get any sleep anyway.'

'Why? Am I crowding you? I can move—' She moved to give him space, but he pulled her back.

'Don't go. Just stay here,' he said, pulling her tighter to him.

They stayed like that, both unable to sleep yet too tired to do anything else but listen to each other's heartbeat. It was a comfortable kind of silence, lying here with his arms around her body, her arms around his waist, her ears against his chest, his chin on her head. It felt so warm and safe to be held like this that her body was falling asleep even as she fought hard not to, wanting to stay conscious long enough to memorize this forever. She could tell that he felt the same way, too, until . . .

The silence was interrupted by her phone vibrating on the bedside table behind her.

He looked up over her head and saw just enough of the phone screen lighting up that it made him frown.

And just like that, the spell was broken, and he pulled away from her, lying on his back with his forearm on his eyes.

She was afraid to look at the screen and find out what could have pulled him away from her with such hurry that she'd think her skin was on fire.

'You should get that, Buttercup. Either someone's dead or dying for him to text you at this ungodly hour.' He didn't say that spitefully, though the words were meant to deliver the same feeling. He was only contemplative, forlorn maybe, but definitely wistful, like he'd been given a taste of sugar for the first time only to be given salt when he asked for it again.

The vibrating had died down before she could answer it, but she got to it long enough to see the name and face on the screen. Nick. Wishing her a good night. Making plans with her. Hoping her day went well. Reminding her of the gig she'd promised she'd go to. She put her phone back on the table without replying, and instead lay there on her back next to someone she really wanted to hold close to her body again. It was like they were a galaxy apart again.

'We're just friends,' she said, her voice cracking.

Kip didn't answer, but he did take his arm off his eyes, which were staring up at her particularly uninteresting off-white ceiling.

'He's been trying to get back with me for months after we broke up, but I know for sure that it's over between us. I told him so.'

Still no answer, and her body ached with the knowledge that she was losing Kip before she even had him.

'I thought, maybe if we became friends, he'd stop thinking that we could still be together—like you and your ex.'

At that, he finally faced her, turning on his side, that valley between his brows appearing again.

She turned to her side to face him back, and the way he was looking at her told her just how wrong she was about him. 'You regret it, your breakup, not trying to win her back, don't you?'

He shook his head, his face softening again against her pillows, and he tucked a stray strand of her hair behind her ear. 'It's not regret. It's not like I had a choice in the matter. I was the second choice. It was . . . ' He ran his fingers through his hair, this time unable to look at her in the face, in her eyes, shame washing over his own face. 'It's grief. Grief for what I lost. Not her. Not any more. I couldn't help feeling like I let my entire life slip away from my hands—a house, a family, children. All because I was only good enough to be second choice.'

She cupped his face in her palm, forcing him to look at her, a new understanding of Kip making a place for itself in her mind, in her heart. It was why he was working so hard. It was why he loved books so much. It was all he had that kept him here. And if he lost it, he'd have nothing else tethering him here. He suddenly felt like sand in the palm of her hand, slipping slowly, slowly away from her hands.

She wrapped her arms around his body, tight and secure and safe, telling him that this was her choice, that he was her first choice with her body, mind, and soul, telling him that she wasn't ready to lose him yet. At least not tonight when the cold crept up between them, held at bay by their shared warmth.

Chapter 18

Crisis Point

The week before the international book fair was always a quiet lull, a time to catch their breaths before the big event, at least for the editors. The eye of the storm, they called it. All books should have been submitted to the printer at least the week before, and they were just waiting for the inventory to be delivered to the warehouse.

Kip had taken to staying over at Emma's place during those peak days when they were rushing to submit files to the printer, but both had been too tired to continue what they had started a few weeks ago, nothing past touching and fondling and kissing, none of the pornographic things that Emma had wanted Kip to do to her and her to him.

Still, it was nice just being with Kip, holding him all through the night and waking up next to him in her bed.

She could still feel his hesitation there, the sudden pulling away whenever her phone lit up to show Nick's name on her screen, either for a call or a message. Kip thought she didn't catch the slight frown, the wavering doubt, the fear on his face whenever Emma picked up Nick's call.

Janey had told her that Kip needed the assurance that she was choosing him, that she wanted only him without a shadow of a doubt.

'I think you should meet Nick,' Emma told Kip one night, the night after they'd finished everything they should have finished for the book fair and he was going home with her to her apartment, walking hand-in-hand along the walkway leading there.

He stopped abruptly, pulling at her hand to stop her from walking ahead of him. 'Why?' There was a sharp accusation in the tone of his voice.

She thought about her answer carefully. She knew that these were dangerous waters she was treading. 'I don't know . . . So, you could beat him up, finally get that off your chest?'

'Emma,' he said, signalling that this was no joking matter.

'I just don't want you to doubt me any more.'

'I . . . ' he began to say, hesitant to finish the rest. 'I don't want you to feel like you have to prove yourself to me.'

'I don't have to . . . ' She stepped up to him, wrapping her palm over the back of his neck, making him slouch slightly to meet her height. 'I *want* to, Kip.'

'Won't it be weird?'

She nudged his nose with hers, lips slightly grazing the side of his mouth. 'Why would it be? He's just my friend.'

Though the doubt was still there in his eyes, he nodded and kissed her, a sign of his agreement.

***

As Emma led Kip into the dark bar where Nick played his gigs, a sinking feeling came to her like acid burning away at her insides. She didn't dare let go of his hand.

The bar was crowded with people who wore black shirts bearing the name of Nick's indie-rock band, Word Warlords, and who were most definitely in many stages of drunk.

Kip and Emma stood at the side, near the bar, feeling and looking out of place in their cardigans and khakis and sweater vests. Then, with both agreeing that it might help them blend in if they were drunk too, Kip went to dive into the crowded bar to order them beer, leaving her alone in that dark corner to wait—and really stay away from the mosh pit of people.

'I knew I'd find you here,' a familiar voice whispered into her ear.

She turned around and saw Nick leaning on the wall next to her, smiling at her in a much too familiar way that he knew shouldn't. After she had explicitly told him that he shouldn't.

'Oh, hi, Nick,' she said, trying not to sound startled. She backed away from him, moving far enough so that she couldn't smell the scent of cigarette smoke and stale alcohol on him. He just closed the gap again. 'I was just waiting for Kip. He went to get us beer at the bar.'

Nick frowned, practically glared at her. 'Kip? The nerd from your office? What's he doing here?'

'I asked him to come with me,' Emma said like it was the most obvious answer in the world. She caught sight of Kip walking back to her with two beer bottles in one hand. 'There he is.'

He slinked an arm around her waist when he got to her, and she did the same to him. 'Kip, you remember Nick, right?'

'I remember him,' Kip said, jaw clenching, the dark anger beginning to spark in his eyes as he stared down Nick. 'Everything good here, bro?'

'All good, *bro*,' Nick said, matching his glare only for a moment before softening his expression for Emma. 'I'm glad you came. Stay and listen to my new song, okay, Ems?'

Emma nodded but was caught by surprise when he cupped her cheek with his palm before walking away towards the stage where his band was waiting for him. Kip didn't say anything, but the grip of his hand on her waist said everything that Emma needed to know. He was right. This was weird. Janey was right. This was a bad idea.

'Let's go home, Kip,' she said, prodding him to the exit. 'We're much too nerdy for this crowd.' He didn't protest and left the untouched beer bottles on the bar on the way to the door.

But they were forced to stop just as they approached the doorway by the spotlight shining down at them.

'This is a song I wrote for my soulmate,' Nick crooned into his mic, the guitar swinging from the strap hanging around his body. 'It's called "The Orbit of our Galaxies." I hope you like it, Emma.'

They were frozen on the spot, forced to stay and listen to Nick sing about second chances and love stories and choosing love even when the infatuation was gone. It should have been romantic. Emma could tell that it was meant to be romantic, but everything about it only made her feel cheated on, coerced into a romantic scene she didn't want to be a part of.

And worst of all, she had dragged Kip with her to this.

Nick made her insides crawl with a fury that she never knew she was capable of feeling, and as the song progressed, Emma got a moment of blissful clarity. She had been a naïve, oblivious, cruel little bitch. Janey was right. Why had it taken her so long to realize that she'd been punishing Nick in this way—and Kip, too.

This was the last straw, and she didn't give Nick the chance to finish his song, to make his case, to fight for what they had lost. It was gone. It was done. It was a black hole. Emma had moved on. And Nick should learn to do so, too.

She left the bar with Kip and brought him home, back to their orbit, back to the galaxy they had been building together.

Chapter 19

Book Fair

Emma felt like a different version of herself when she was around Kip. Like she was wearing that dress she'd been saving for a special occasion. Like she was wearing bright red lipstick on a rainy day. Like she was wearing new shoes that fit so perfectly she wondered why she'd ever thought it was going to hurt before it got better. She fitted better in her life. She felt better, looked better if the way Kip looked at her was to be believed. It was still her in there, so completely herself, and yet different. Good different.

This must be what a makeover felt like, that trope so popular in earlier romances where the protagonist was transformed with makeup, haircut, fashionable clothes, and a good talk-down by her best friend about why she was so pretty, especially without her glasses on. Maybe it was a combination of both form and essence. Making an effort to look good and feel good about herself and reaping the extra benefit of Kip staring longingly at her first thing in the morning.

Not that he looked at her any differently in her oversized, ratty *Star Wars* sleeping shirt. Or at midnight when the mascara had smudged around her eyes. Or now, in a denim jumper, as she helped stock shelves, bag book purchases, and track lines in their booth at the country's biggest book selling event of the year.

On the first day, right before they'd opened their booth, as the books they'd been working on for months were being delivered to the stock rooms while the booth was being set up, Kip stood next to her with the editorial staff, watching and waiting for the culmination of their hard work to unfold, here, now. The booth was about twenty to thirty square feet of space in a large event exhibit hall and was walled in by tarpaulin printed with patterns of their book catalogue this year held up by metal frames. To one side were the cash registers and in the very middle was a table of books still hot from the printing presses. And on every wall were shelves and shelves of books, new and old, waiting for readers to take them home.

This was always Emma's favourite part of the job, seeing the books for the first time after all the hard work, holding it in her hands, feeling it still hot against her skin, watching readers pick up the books that she'd loved the first time she found them. All those months of working from daylight to midnight melted away with the exhaustion, and she was just a puddle of joy. Sometimes, she'd even tear up a little when she stared at the wall of books.

An arm slinked over her shoulder and pulled her to him, her side pressing to his. 'Well, Buttercup, we did it. We birthed all these books just in time for the book fair.' He held out a white handkerchief for her.

She dabbed the handkerchief on her cheeks. 'Have you seen anything more beautiful?' she asked, still staring at the wall of books.

He smiled, his hand on her shoulder squeezing her skin, his face in her hair, lips whispering into her ear. 'I could think of a couple of things.'

Someone cleared her throat behind them, startling Emma into pushing Kip away from her. Janey was staring at them with an eyebrow quirked upward directed at Emma, grip tight on her iPad. Their other coworkers were stealing glances at them, too, as they worked though not as blatantly or intensely as Janey.

'Alegre, production needs you in the stock room. They have questions about that non-fiction journalism book,' she said, casting a quick look at Kip before turning her attention back to her best friend. 'Emma, you stay here.'

'I'll see you later, Buttercup,' Kip said, patting the small of Emma's back as he passed her on the way to the stockroom.

She followed him with her eyes as he walked away. When she turned back to Janey, she startled back. Her best friend was standing so close to her, her face was right up in front of her. 'Okay, Buttercup, this thing you have with Kip *and* Nick, that's a powder keg waiting to explode.' Emma took a couple of steps back to impose personal space, her hands raised in front of her to stop her best friend. Janey took Emma's wrist and closed the gap again. 'In your face, Emma. It's gonna explode in your face.'

'Nothing is going on between us, Janey. Check your chill, girl. The week's gonna be busy for you,' Emma said.

'Between who, Emma?' Janey said. 'Kip? Nick? You and Nick are getting way too friendly again—'

'That's over! I ended it!'

'Nope! You two have too much history. Exes can never be friends. And all these weekend lunch dates and chatting, it's not good for both of you if Kip is in the picture.'

'If this is about the coach again—'

'Theo's old news. I'm already seeing someone new. And don't evade the topic, Emma. You're working up the nerve to get back together with Nick?'

'No! It's really over between me and Nick. I've blocked him on all my social media and erased his contact details on my phone. I broke it off completely.'

'Make sure Nick knows that.'

'Nick and I, we have history. But that's all that is left of it. History. I know he was my best friend before—'

'Girl, I'm your best friend. And Kip? What is this thing between you and Kip?'

Emma's jaw dropped, her mind blanking. She definitely wanted something to happen between her and Kip, but whenever she tried, he wouldn't let her in, not completely, not since Nick sang her that stupid song. Sometimes, she thought he was about to say that he wanted her, that he wanted her so much that it hurt, but then he would always pull away as if the thought hadn't occurred to him, and as if she didn't notice.

Janey was waiting for her to answer with the expectant, patient look that she'd worn back when Emma was bawling about her breakup with Nick. It was how Emma knew that Janey could see through her lie. Her best friend was not a particularly patient person.

'Honest to goodness, I don't know, Janey,' Emma said, pressing the heels of her palm on her closed eyelids. 'Kip sleeps over at my place when we have to work late nights, and we get intimate, but we never go all the way. It's like there's a wall between us that he's hesitant to jump over. But when we're together it's like nothing else exists but him and me.'

'Kip's not the kind who likes losing, I told you. In all the years we've worked at the company, the guy's never done anything half-baked. Especially not in matters of the heart,' Janey said, looking as if she had something more to add, but held back. 'He hates competition, and he especially hates being the underdog.'

Emma narrowed her eyes suspiciously at her best friend. 'What aren't you telling me, Janey?'

'I'm saying he only plays if he knows he'll win.'

Emma groaned, rolled her eyes, and raised her hands in surrender. 'That is a vaguely aggressive way of saying he doesn't like being rejected. That's not an exclusive feeling. But what else do I have to do? I'm practically throwing myself at him.'

Janey stared at her friend, trying to read her mannerisms, her face, her eyes, and then shaking her head as if coming to a revelation that she should have seen all along. She put her iPad down on the display table. 'You're falling for Kip, aren't you?' Janey said.

Emma lowered her hands, her shoulders slumping as if her friend had taken a weight off her shoulders and had finally noticed how exhausted she was from carrying all that weight. Janey knew just what her friend needed. She pulled Emma into a hug.

Emma buried her face in Janey's neck, saying, 'I think so. I don't understand what's stopping him.'

Janey pulled away to look her friend in the eyes. 'Maybe he's hesitating because of Nick?'

Emma considered that in her head, staring back at her friend who seemed to know all the answers to her questions. 'Kip is not like you. He actually thinks that exes can be friends.'

Janey narrowed her suspicious eyes at Emma. 'Does he? Do you?'

Speakers screeched all over the exhibit area, signalling the start of the day and the wave of customers coming to the booths. Janey pressed her palm on Emma's shoulder, apologetically and reassuringly as if she had given Emma the answer she needed. Still, when she saw Kip again for the rest of the five-day event, she felt both good and bad, both so completely herself and so confused at the same time.

Chapter 20

Take Me Home

The book fair ended in a celebratory mood. Five days zipped past fast for the company, but to Emma, it felt like honey dripping so agonizingly slowly that she couldn't get in the same mood as her coworkers.

Many of their books sold out. Many of the new books were best-sellers—Kip's graphic novels and non-fiction books, Emma's romances, and even Jesse's weird, novelty TikTok books. The total sales for the entire five days made a serious contribution to their yearly revenue targets. Brent was so happy that he offered to take the entire company to dinner that night, which was met with tired groans. Everybody just wanted to go home, collapse on their beds, and sleep until next week.

Not Emma, who was still reeling from her talk with Janey four days ago. And certainly not Kip, who had asked her out to a late dinner that night before driving her home.

In his car, her heart was a storm cloud heavy with rain that refused to fall. She stole sidelong glances at Kip, who was humming to a song that played on the speaker. Janey's question had echoed in the chambers of her mind throughout those gruelling five days. Did he? Did he know? Did Kip know that it's him she wants?

'All right, Buttercup, you've been an ogre these past five days.' Kip had slowly but surely become so attuned to her moods, her feelings, her heart that he could tell with one quick look that something was bothering her—a skill that could give Janey a run for her money. 'Tell me what's bothering you.'

'Does it still bother you that I tried to be friends with my ex? That I have history with him?' she blurted out, and immediately, it created an open space in her chest that was quickly filled with dread. What if she didn't like his answer?

His jaw clenched, that crease between his brows deepening, clearly not expecting to be confronted with this right now. He was taking his time to answer her, and now she wondered how she could have thought that the last five days were slow when this, here, now, waiting in agony for him to answer felt like lightyears. 'Tell me what you really want, Emma.'

'That's not the answer to my question, Kip.' She faced him fully, tilting her body under the seat belt. Her eyes could have burnt holes in him from the intense feeling burning in the back of her eyeballs.

His hands gripped the wheel tight, unwilling to let go of control, unwilling to risk looking at her and seeing on her face the answer to his question. 'That's not the answer to *my* question, Emma.'

She felt doors closing on her face from that answer. 'I don't want you to take me to dinner. I want you to take me home.'

'Okay,' he said with a sad sigh, clicking the light to make a U-turn. 'I'll drive you back to your condo.'

'No, Kip.' She placed a firm hand on his forearm. 'I want you to take me *home*.'

Kip still didn't look at her, the signal lights of his car still blinking, the stoplight ahead beginning to loom over them in the small space of his car. He'd let her in as far as he was willing to risk, and now Emma wanted more. She wanted all of him. The question was if he wanted her too. The question was if he believed that she was telling him the truth. The question was if his doubt was more powerful than his wanting of her.

When the stoplight turned green, he turned the signal lights off and took her home.

***

Emma walked along the walls, bookshelves, and mantles that held the gallery of his life. From childhood to adulthood, she noted the way time had changed him, moulded him into the man she knew today.

Kip's home was a typical Filipino upper-middle-class home. It was a two-storey neo-vernacular structure built on a slope on the hills of Antipolo with an expansive view of the city below. All around the house were mountains and cliffs and long stretches of empty roads that felt emptier as the night deepened. Now she understood why he would spend so much on gas money just to go to work every day. It must be unbelievably lonely living here alone.

Kip was in the kitchen, preparing tea, and thankfully buying both of them time to work up the nerve to ask the questions they both needed answers to.

What did they want from each other?

A family photo was the centrepiece of the gallery, taking the position of honour over the mantle directly facing the door. He had an older brother (the doctor) and a younger brother (the lawyer), whose graduation photos were displayed on the walls with their many medals and certificates. He had his father's build and bone structure, the crease between his brows, all the hard parts of Kip that made him seem so stoic, so unapproachable came from his father. But she saw where

Kip's soft parts came from, his gentle brown eyes, the curls of his dark brown hair, the easy, heart-fluttering smile, the dimples—all of it came from his mother. His brothers were mostly their father's, but him, he was his mother's. Next, she stared at a row of baby photos and she immediately recognized Kip. He'd had that crease on his forehead all this time. It wasn't a wrinkle from frowning all the time. There were other photos from different places, different ages, different times. In fact, many of the photos were set in New Zealand. She tried her best to commit the best ones of Kip to memory. She stopped at a photo of Kip set in Hobbiton, right in front of Bilbo Baggins's circular door with the brass knocker. He was a lanky teenager smiling from ear to ear and wearing an oversized, black *The Lord of The Rings* movie poster shirt.

'Before you say anything, I didn't actually live in Hobbiton when we lived in New Zealand years ago,' Kip said, his usual humour back in his tone, strolling back from the kitchen and into the living room. He set two mugs down on the coffee table in front of the couch and plopped into it with a tired groan. 'Believe it or not, Buttercup, I'm not actually a Hobbit.'

'No, you're too tall. An Ent maybe. Just look at how tall you were at—were you fifteen here?' she said, holding his Hobbiton photo up to him.

He smiled. 'Thirteen actually.'

'Wow. Thank your dad's genes for the bone structure then,' she said, turning away from his gaze as she set the photo back down on the mantle.

'Come sit with me, Emma—' he said when she was taking too long. 'I made us chamomile tea.'

Emma drew in a deep breath and walked back to the couch, accepting the mug of hot tea that Kip handed to her, wishing it was something stronger. She pressed her lips up to the rim, but didn't drink, her eyes still on the gallery of Kip's life. 'I feel like I don't know you, Kip. How long did you live in New Zealand again?'

'Just a few years, with trips back to here from time to time. The entire family migrated there. Dad was a diplomat, and we spent almost a decade in New Zealand until mom decided that it was time we established roots in our homeland. We stayed until my brothers graduated and passed their bar and medical exams,' Kip said, following her line of sight as he sipped on his own tea.

'And they're all living there now? Why did you stay here?'

'I did try to live there again for a year before I started working at the publishing house. First world country. Better opportunities. Better healthcare. Better quality of life. My brothers are doing really well there. But me? I'm not a doctor or a lawyer. I don't even have the skills to become a diplomat like my dad or a teacher like mom. I liked that I was with my family, but I jumped from one dead end job after another. I didn't feel like myself. Like I was a different person, and I wasn't sure if I liked that person. When I returned here, it was only supposed to be for a vacation, time to figure out what I wanted with my life while I cleaned up our affairs here. You know, sell the house, pack our valuables and photos that we left behind, then go back to New Zealand for good.'

'And then you found books?' Emma interjected, feeling Kip's eyes on her back as she leaned forward to place the mug on the table and then leaned back into the coach to meet Kip's gentle, liquid eyes in the lowlights of the living room. His eyes were so comforting, so ardent that her heart could burst in her chest any time, and she still wouldn't let herself look away. 'You do know me,' Kip said, taking her hand on the couch and intertwining her fingers with his. 'I haven't left since.'

Emma stole one glance at their intertwined hands, noting just how good, how right, how perfect his big hands felt in hers. 'So why not find a job there where you get to make books for living?'

Kip put down his mug on the coffee table and tilted his body so he was facing her. He didn't let go of her hand the entire time. 'If I didn't know better, I'd think you're trying to deport me, Buttercup.'

'Your family's there. It makes sense, doesn't it?'

He leaned into the back of the couch. She copied his posture so that they were face to face, hands holding the other's tightly.

'I've thought about it, but every time I work up the nerve to join my family, life gives me reasons to stay,' he said, suddenly tracing the outline of her cheek and her jaw with the fingers of his free hand, then cupping her cheek in his warm palm.

She pressed her cheek into his palm to show him just how right and perfect every part of her fits into him. 'Aren't you lonely?'

'Right now?' He shook his head slowly, gaze piercing into her own eyes. 'Not at all, Buttercup.' His thumb made slow circular strokes on the back of her hand.

'Tell me. Does it bother you that I tried to be friends with my ex?'

'Emma . . . '

'Just please answer me.'

'You have history with him. What chance do I have against that? Why did you break up with him anyway?'

'We just drifted apart during the lockdown. He was dealing with his own dark stuff, and my mother died in the first year of the pandemic. There were just too many things going on in my life—mama's sickness and death, her medical bills, my day job, his issues—and I thought I would only be cruel to myself if I tried to fix us when I was so broken myself. I knew for sure that I didn't love him the way he needed me to love him. So, I broke up with him.'

'But you kept him in your life after that anyway?'

'Not until he pulled that stunt at the bar did I realize that the kinder thing to do was to break it off with him completely.'

When he didn't answer her for a long time, she scooched closer to him so that her thigh touched his and placed her palm on his neck to pull him closer to her. 'Why can't you see that I want you so much, Kip? Every bit of me aches for you. My skin burns to touch you. You live in my dreams and when I wake, I could practically see your face in the drowsy haze.'

He pulled her body to him and positioned her to sit on his lap. His hands cupped her face, her hair falling over the back of his hands. 'I'm going to kiss you, Emma.'

'Just do it, Kip,' she said with a roll of her eyes before smothering his lips with hers. She fixed herself on him, straddling him on the couch, and putting her arms around his neck in an attempt to kiss him deeper, harder, more intensely, so desperate she was to prove that it was only him she wanted. Only him.

Gasping, she pulled away to speak, while his lips drew a line down her jaw, her neck, her throat, her shoulders.

'Let me get the condoms in my bag,' she said, attempting weakly to pull away and reach into her bag.

'No need. I have some in my room,' he said with his lips on hers, wrapping his arms around her body, and he stood up from the couch, carrying her to his room.

'See? We're not such big dorks after all,' she said, ravishing him as he walked.

He laughed. 'I do know a happy ending that you really, really, really want.'

Chapter 21

Love Scene

Emma had trouble separating this love scene with Kip from the scenes she escaped into in her head when she was stressing out. Because his hands sliding over her body, his lips marking every inch of her skin, his body experimenting with every way he could fit with her—these were all definitely real.

Where then could she run to if things went wrong with Kip?

Kip was taking his time with her, dissecting this thing between them with the patience of a book editor. He walked through the threshold of his room, pressing her up against walls, shelves, glass cases along the way as he peeled away layers of her. Her shoes were the first to come off, thrown off haphazardly along the hallway outside his room.

While pressing her up against the door, he slipped her cardigan off her shoulders, letting it fall into a pile at her feet. On a bookshelf, the buttons of her pants unclasped, the zipper going down, and he had to pull away momentarily from her to pull the denim completely off her and then dive back into smothering her with kisses. He pulled her towards a glass case and pulled her shirt over her head, throwing the fabric aside before stepping back, jaw dropping, eyes taking in as much of her as he could.

'Fuck, Emma,' Kip muttered.

She grinned at him. 'That's the idea, Kip.'

Without breaking eye contact with him, she twisted one strap of her bra in her fingers and let it fall down her shoulders so that it rested limply against her forearm. She watched the Adam's apple bob in his throat. She did the same with the other strap and then took his hands to cup her breasts over the fabric.

Placing her palms on his nape, she pulled his face to hers to kiss him slowly, patiently. He answered her kiss, his hands finding their way to the clasp of her bra behind her, fumbling clumsily with the hook as he accidentally bit her bottom lip.

'Ow!' she said against his lips. 'Need help?'

'No, I can do this,' he said still with the patience of a book editor, turning her body around to look at the clasp, leaving her face to face with her reflection on the glass case of toys and action figures. When finally, the bra slipped off her front, he pressed his body against her back, watching his hands sliding over her bare breasts in the reflection of the glass. 'Oh my god, Emma,' he whispered into her ear, eyes on their reflection.

One hand slipped down over her panties, and she wished she'd worn something sexier than the purple Cheshire cat-patterned cotton panties she was wearing. She'd thought it was funny when she bought cat-patterned panties online. She couldn't for the life of her remember why it was funny now. She should have listened to Janey.

She gasped and arched her back when his fingers pressed up against the middle of her folds, her underwear beginning to soak through.

'You're already wet,' he said with his lips on her ear.

'And you're—' She gasped when his fingers began a slow and steady rub between her folds, 'not naked!' The words came out as deep gasps for breath. His free hand pressed at her stomach, pushing her body to fit in his as he rolled his hips over her back, his already hard sex pressing up on the back of her thigh, her legs close to giving up under her. She reached one arm over her shoulder to hold on to him—if it was to hold him or to stay upright, she couldn't tell any more. Her other hand went to slip his hand under her panties, setting the tone, the pitch, the rhythm that she wanted his fingers to play on her. She watched her reflection unravel under Kip's hands and when his finger dipped into her, she let out a sound that was part scream, part gasp for breath, part his name. But it was the look on Kip's face that unmade her completely. Loving. Hungry. Wanting. Earnest. So perfectly fitting with her body. It took all of her not to close her eyes and dance to the story he was writing on her skin.

Just as she reached the pinnacle of her pleasure, he unravelled her again in another way—just as he had done with every interaction with her. He turned her to him and kissed her deeply, slowly pushing her to sit on the bed. He parted her legs and knelt in the space between, his face level with hers, pausing right there to stare into her eyes.

'You're so beautiful, Emma,' he said, tucking stray strands of her hair behind her ears and then cupping her cheeks.

'Let's do something you want to do.' She pulled his glasses off his face and leaned down to kiss him softly, tenderly on the lips, and then broke the kiss to pull his shirt off him. The moment it was off, he kissed her again, more intensely this time, pushing her to lie down with her legs dangling off the side of the bed. He crawled over her, lips, teeth, tongue writing poetry on her body. With his hands on her hips, he hovered over her breasts and looked at her as he took one into his mouth, flicking the nipple with his tongue. She arched her body to him, her thighs forced open wider with his massive body still lodged between her legs. He moved further down till he was face to face with her purple, not-funny-any more Cheshire-Cat-patterned underwear, staring at the space between her legs, a smile coming to his lips. 'Okay. You win,' he said with a laugh.

She propped herself up on her elbows. 'What?'

'You're the queen of book references. I won't challenge you again, pussy cat,' he said, grinning at her, slipping her panties almost too reverently down her legs, and then diving into her before she could answer.

Kip licked her, the pad of his tongue staying there and flicking up and down. She let out a surprised gasp as she fell back into the pillows, her head nestled in the fabric, as her body arched from the magic Kip was making with his mouth and tongue. She pushed herself up to her elbows again to watch him, her entire body trembling from the force of him.

'Kip, I want you,' she said, half begging, half commanding.

He looked up from the number he was doing on her and said against her, 'Not yet,' before inserting a finger, the one callused by red pens, reaching into the pinnacle of her. His other hand pressed on her stomach, pushing her to lie back down on the bed and then cupping her breast.

'Kip!' she screamed his name, intending to tell him something important—something that she forgot when her own name passed his lips.

She grabbed a handful of his hair, her other hand digging into his shoulders for support. 'Kip, I want you. Now.' There was a feral quality in the way she commanded him to come to her, a growl that reverberated from the warm pit of her stomach crawling up to her throat.

He pulled away from her, and she drew in a deep breath as if she had been holding her breath the whole time.

Kip crawled on top of her, propping himself up on his elbows on either side of her, knees still keeping her open to him. He pulled her legs around his waist and caressed her cheek with the back of his hand, pausing to look at her, really look at her with eyes burdened by a million questions that were jostling to be asked. Only one question did matter. 'Are you sure, Emma?' he asked, the uncertainty there breaking her heart. 'Are you sure I'm the one you want?'

It was as if Emma was thrown into icy waters, the breath still frozen in her chest. She wondered if love, or at least the beginnings of it, was ever this uncertain and so perennially unassuming of its existence in a person's heart. She wondered if this, what she was feeling for him now, was love. She was so sure that she wanted Kip so much that she could not remember a time when she didn't want him. Not when she first saw him in the office when she was applying for the editor job. Not when they fought over the dumbest things like paper and manuscript edits and literary references. Not now, when all she wanted was to pull him closer to her body, as close as she could have him, as close as he would let him.

I think I love him, she thought, and the admission in her mind was the water's surface broken, the breath of fresh air. *I love him.*

She wrapped her arms around his shoulders, pulling him down to her—her bare breasts on his chest, his hips on top of hers, his mint-chocolate breath on her cheek—desperate to feel his weight on her body, and nodded. 'I want you, Kip. It's only ever been you.'

She glimpsed a sliver of joy spark behind his eyes, and Kip kissed her deeply, minus the desperation, minus the uncertainty, minus the fear. He pulled away momentarily from her, pulled out a foil packet from the drawer of the bedside table, and ripped it open with his teeth. Emma pulled his pants down for him and helped him put on birth control.

He positioned himself at her sex, and smiling, he said, 'Don't break my heart, Emma.'

There was a pause, a stillness that could almost burn paper skin. She felt his heart pounding against her chest, her body drumming with anticipation against his.

She gasped for breath when he pushed all the way in, filling her so deliciously and completely, and she dug her fingernails into his back. They stayed like that, eyes not breaking contact as their bodies got used to this sensation, this coalescence of body, mind, and soul. The rhythm of her heart became his. The pattern of his breath became hers. The warmth of their skins intertwined as if from one body. Both exhaled satisfying breaths.

Kip smiled at her, breaking any more walls between them. 'Hi, Buttercup.'

And she opened up to him, giggling like a lovesick schoolgirl falling in love for the first time. 'Hi, Hobbit.'

He rolled his hips over her, and she clenched around him, letting out a sound that was both a whimper and a moan at the same time. Inside her, he pulsed and thrummed and pushed her walls that pushed back. He rolled his hips again, this time more in tune to her body, to the way she reacted to him. He grew more daring with every thrust, pulling out far enough that she felt like a chunk of her was torn apart from her, a hint of loss, of the void, of life without the other, only to go back in again, returning what was thought to be lost.

Soon, all semblance of control was thrown out the window, the world melted away, and it was just them floating, flying, soaring, their names filling the air with their every breath.

Emma reached so high up and out the troposphere, stratosphere, mesosphere, and thermosphere of this physical realm, screaming Kip's name all the way out to the farther frontiers of the galaxies, with Kip not so far behind her, two comets that dared break through the skies and fell into the quiet, peaceful void of space.

He fell on top of her, pressing his lips against her neck, and saying her name between deep, ragged breaths, 'Emma, Emma, Emma.' The first an expression of contentment, then gratitude, then joy. She imagined the last, the one that was barely audible, barely a whisper, like a secret that refused to be revealed, to be an expression of love. She kept her arms around him, holding him as close as she could, holding him as if refusing to let go of him yet, as if afraid he'd let go of her too soon.

And she thought this must be what a happy ending felt like. A daydream given flesh and bones and weight in her arms. A reality that felt too much like a dream she could escape to when she was wide awake.

Chapter 22

Wildest Fantasies

Waking up next to a lover in the aftermath of a love scene always had a dream-like quality to it in stories. Sunlight streamed through thin curtains, falling on a lover's face like a sepia photo faded over time. A gentle quiet fell over the setting, like a cloud, a pillow, soft fabric floating in the room. Time rode the rhythms of their heartbeats, slow and tender and steady, after a night that felt like a fever dream. Two bodies tangled in each other, the pull of reality mercifully reluctant to separate them so fast when the two were one just hours ago.

Emma thought she was still dreaming when she woke up with Kip's arm around her body, her cheek on his chest, his heartbeat drumming calmly, slowly in her ears. This was a scene in a romance. They were replaying scenes in romances. Unconsciously. Unironically. But surely not insincerely.

She stared up in wonder at his face, eyes still closed, lips slightly parted, his floppy hair flat over his brow, lashes feathering softly on his cheeks. This was a new side of him that she'd never seen. Vulnerable and so unguarded that he caught her off-guard when his hand slid from her shoulder and settled on her waist, startling her.

'What are you thinking, Buttercup?' he asked, voice low, airy, coarse the way sand was coarse before the ocean softened it in a blanket of its water. He cracked open one eye to look at her. 'You have that weird smile again. The one you make when a scene in a book you're editing is spicy.'

'I was just thinking how this scene could be plucked out of a romance novel.'

He let out a laugh. 'And we're like hyper self-aware characters in a book?'

'Yeah. Just two nerds standing in the middle of a nerdy joke.'

The corner of his lip quirked upward, another laugh reverberating from his throat. 'You mean lying naked next to each other in the middle of a joke?' he said, wrapping his other arm around her, pulling her close, his lips buried in her hair on top of her head.

Emma grinned at him. 'We can still make the joke a dirty joke if you want.'

'Emma! It's Monday,' he said, rolling them over so that he was on top of her. 'We'll have to be quick. We have work to do.'

'Ugh! Who brings up work before sex?' she said, burying her face in the crook of his neck.

She felt his laugh come from the very base of his stomach where her sex pressed up to his torso, and she buried her hands in his hair while his hands were on her hips.

'You're right. What was I thinking? Let's take the day off. Or better yet, let's just not go to work forever and fuck each other till we die of hunger or till the zombie apocalypse knocks down my bedroom door. Whichever comes first.'

'Yippee-ki-yay, motherfucker,' she said.

He propped himself up on his elbows so that he could look at her face, fingers tucking stray hair behind her ears. 'That's not a book reference, Buttercup.'

'If I remember correctly, Hobbit, you said I'm the queen of book references and you will never challenge me again.'

'Not fair. I was losing my mind over you when I said that...'
He trailed off, staring lovingly at her face, ready to surrender
everything to her if she'd asked...

'What? What is it, Kip?' She pulled herself up so she was
partly leaning back into the headboard, dragging Kip with her.
He took his time answering her, eyes searching her face for...
assurance? She wasn't sure. She let him take his time.

Their new position gave her a better view of the glass case
display full of science fiction and fantasy action figures and
bookshelves containing books of every shape, size, edition, and
genre. They said a bookshelf was a glimpse into a person's soul
and looking at Kip's collection—new paperbacks with cracked
spines, hardcovers with colourful dust jackets, and leather-
bound books in glass cases, from Kipling, Tolkien, Herbert,
Brontë, and Austen to Jordan, Erikson, Butcher, Sanderson,
and Weeks—was like looking at a prism in the light. Every
angle different. Every surface as dazzling as the others. She
imagined running her fingers along the spines as if she were
counting the bones on Kip's own vertebrae.

He shook his head, his five o'clock shadow lightly scratching
her skin. 'Nothing.'

'Come on!' She slapped her hands on his cheek and
squeezed. 'It's never nothing if it makes the wrinkle between
your brows go down that deep.' She poked at the crease, then
smoothed it out with her thumb.

'It's just...' He let out a nervous breath. 'I never thought
I'd find myself here with you, Emma.'

'And I never thought I'd ever find myself in the nerdiest
bedroom ever.'

'Now, who's the buzzkill?' He flicked her forehead lightly.
'I was baring my heart out to you. I thought a romance expert
like you would recognize that we were having a moment.'

'We were. It's just hard to focus with Gandalf the Grey and Yoda watching us.' Emma pointed at the action figures. 'You made me stare at them while you unhooked my bra!' She laughed.

'Compared to Darcy, Wentworth, and Knightley literally jumping on your bed when we're getting busy?'

'My cats like you more than they like me. So really, it's your fault. They were protecting you from me.'

'It bodes well for me that your cats like me.'

She rolled her eyes in jest. 'Those ingrates. I feed them every day and I've raised them since they were kittens. Let me meet your parents. I'll make them love me more than they love you.'

'Oh, I don't think you'll need to try so hard. I'm sure they'll love you when they meet you,' he said.

'Really? Why?'

'My parents are the biggest book nerds and they love meeting other book nerds. They named all their children after their favourite authors. They even have the nerdiest meet-cute story.'

'Oooh! Tell me! Tell me!' She rolled them over so she was on top of him. 'I love a good meet-cute!'

He smiled, his thumbs making gentle strokes on her hip. 'They met at their university library. Papa was being sent to India at the time for work and wanted to read up on Rudyard Kipling's experience there. Mama was researching colonial literature with a focus on Kipling for graduate school. They touched hands when they were reaching for the same copy of *The Light That Failed* from the bookshelf. They named me after the author. Well, the name was supposed to go to Kuya Ron, but a relative got in the way. So, I was the second choice for the name.'

'Wait. Wait. Hold up! Your full name is Rudyard Kipling Alegre?'

'And your full name is Emma Elizabeth Morales. What gives, Buttercup?' Him knowing her full name made the butterflies in her stomach flutter.

'You have the dorkiest name ever, Hobbit.'

'You should hear my brothers'. Ronald Reuel Tolkien and Raymond Richard Martin.'

'No way!' She laughed out loud.

'What? Papa was reading George R.R. Martin before he became "American Tolkien". And Mama studied Tolkien for graduate school. They were book nerds before it was cool to be a nerd.'

'And so are you!'

'I would say the same thing to you. When I first saw you, you were reading Goldman's version of *The Princess Bride* in the lobby of the office, and I thought I've never seen a book nerd as hot as you.'

'I remember you from that day.' She drew circles on his skin. 'I was interviewing for the junior editor job. You were wearing a black shirt with *The Hobbit* movie poster printed on the front.'

'It was *The Lord of the Rings* shirt. *The Hobbit* movie is what happens when money people meddle in the creative process.'

'You mean movie blockbusters?'

'Whatever! Point is, before the lockdown, I'd been working up the nerve to ask you out on a date for months. Then I found out you have a boyfriend and I just backed off.'

She tilted her head to the side, a thought popping up in her head as she looked into his eyes. 'You do that a lot.'

'Do what?'

'When you think you don't have a fighting chance or when you sense that you're losing, you back off almost immediately. We all thought you had a concussion when you started barking orders at us at the company sports tournaments.'

'It's not like I'm gonna try to steal you away from your boyfriend like a psycho stalker.'

'Ex-boyfriend, Kip. Ex,' she said, leaning close to his face. 'Besides, you only pick fights when it's about books or with me, which now that I think about it, I'm not sure if I should take as a compliment or if I should take offence.'

'I think, subconsciously, I was trying to make you pay attention to me,' he said with a sheepish laugh. 'It feels like a schoolyard game in hindsight, doesn't it?'

'But you did ask me out eventually.' She propped herself up with her elbows on his chest. 'What changed your mind?'

'Your *Star Wars* sleeping shirt,' he said with a laugh, cupping her right boob. 'You were so nerdy and cute and sexy in it with your dorky glasses, the hair bun on top of your head, and Chewbacca on your boob.'

'Kip!'

'Fine!' He held her face in both hands to look straight at her face. 'When I saw you with your ex that night you rushed back to the office in your sleeping shirt, I thought for sure you'd take him back, and when you told him to go home, I knew that if I didn't shoot my shot soon, I might never get my chance.'

'You waited till Valentine's Day to ask me out!'

'Eh, I'm a sucker for a good love story. Valentine's Day dates. Kissing at midnight. The airport chase. Walking on the beach at sunset.' He turned them over so he was on top again, a mischievous grin blooming on his face. 'Morning after sex with your mascara smudged and your hair bun unravelled and spread out on my pillow.' He lowered his face to hers to kiss her. 'I want them all with you, Emma.'

'Let's go on a trip this weekend? Since we're remaking romance scenes,' Emma said as Kip's lips carved a new path from her lips to her jaw, her earlobes, her neck, going further and further down. Her hands sliding over his back.

'What did you have in mind?'

'Sunset at the beach sounds good,' she said when Kip rolled his hips, pressing himself against the space between her legs, making her gasp out loud the next words. 'Or sex! Lots of it. Sex on the beach!' Kip was already putting on a condom. 'Or anywhere! We can stay here and fuck till the walking dead come!' He rolled his hips to enter her, increasing the tempo faster and faster, thrusting in and out of her in long and slow intervals as if savouring this moment with her this time. Last night, they consumed each other with the hunger of a man stuck in the desert. This was a twelve-course meal. 'Fuck me at the airport. In a coffee shop restroom. In a dumpster! I don't care, Kip, as long as it's you!'

'Buttercup, there isn't a place in the world where we haven't done this in all my wildest fantasies.'

Chapter 23

Daylight

The weekend didn't come fast enough, but when it did, it felt like a movie montage, bits and pieces of scenes strung together to indicate a passage of time.

Suddenly, Emma and Kip were lying on beach chairs under a large umbrella, reading the latest revised draft of *Menagerie* on their tablets.

Kip had been trying to feel her up under her white kaftan dress, but people kept walking so close to them that he couldn't go all the way. So, he settled with holding her hand as they read. Time passed so fast that before they knew it, it was past noon and their stomachs were growling like unleashed beasts.

'I'll go get us something to eat, Buttercup,' Kip said, planting a kiss on top of her head and copping a feel of her boob before going to one of the restaurants lining the beachfront. She watched him walk away, his muscular toned skin exposed to the bright light of day, his beach shorts riding low over his waist that her eyes went to the rise of his ass hidden underneath.

Emma's phone had been vibrating nonstop with message notifications—many of which were from Janey demanding that she tell her every sordid detail of their affair. She and Kip had posted matching photos on the beach this morning, which of course had invited speculation from all their friends, family, coworkers, and authors. In Emma's book, that made Kip and her social media official, which really was another layer of confirmation that Kip needed from her.

One of the notifications was a missed call from Amora, who had been waiting for their comments for the last round of revisions last week. Emma called her back, which was immediately answered with a request for a video call.

'Emma! I'm so happy for you!' Amora screamed, making heart eyes at the camera as if she was talking to Emma in person. 'I can't believe it finally happened!'

Emma narrowed her eyes at the screen. 'Finally? What do you mean finally?'

'There's an ongoing bet among us authors about you two hooking up.' Amora didn't even look like she was sorry they were doing this behind her and Kip's back.

'There is?'

'Yeah, and I won! I bet on you two falling in love and getting happily-ever-after like in the romance classics.'

Of course, the best-selling romance author had bet on happily-ever-after. 'This isn't what I had expected from this call. I really thought you had questions about the last round of edits.'

'*Menagerie?* We're so close to the ending that I've begun to let go of it. Sorry, Ems.'

'But are you happy with the ending?'

'I think so, but you caught me. The ending still feels wonky for me, but I'll work on it with your next round of comments. This happy ending is just more complex than my usual stuff, that's why I'm struggling with it I guess.'

'There are many different ways for an ending to be happy. Just write what feels right to you, Amora.'

'That's the thing. The ending of *Menagerie* feels like the sad kind of happy ending. When I was planning *The Menagerie of Lost Things*, I was thinking about how the past leaves marks and remnants of memory in our hearts, sometimes blocking out new happiness to keep a resemblance of what was once happy—even if these same things don't make us happy any more. When the shard in D:ECEMBE-R's drive was taken out, he was finally able to move on from his past and let MAIA in. Did he really have to lose a part of himself to be happy? Can't we ever move forward, towards other happy endings, without losing our past? The menagerie of lost things is all the things from the past that's holding us back, but it's also parts of us that make us who we are.'

'Exactly. So what use is the past then if it'll block us out from a truly happy life? And how much of it must we let go without fundamentally losing ourselves?'

'Now that is a question that I need to answer for the ending. It's nice to hear it out loud. I couldn't articulate it for a while there until I talked to you.'

'So, do you have an answer for it? For the thematic question of your story?'

Amora shrugged. 'Do *you* have an answer for it?'

The question thrown back at her was like a splash of ice-cold water to the face. Did she have an answer for it? For how much of the past she must let go without losing herself? For what use the past was if it was blocking us out from a truly happy life? For how this story's happy ending must play out?

She thought she'd struggle with the answer, but she didn't. It came to her, as easily inhaling in a fresh breath of ocean air.

'Does Kip have an answer for it?' Amora added, grinning widely at her. Emma's expression on the screen an answer in itself.

'He does,' Kip said, scooching next to Emma on her beach chair, draping an arm over her shoulder and nuzzling his face in her hair.

'Oh my god! Is that Kip? He looks like the Asian Bachelor,' Amora said.

'It's Kip,' Emma said, leaning into Kip's kiss.

'Hi, Amora. Your book is turning out really great,' Kip said.

'Oh my god, that means so much to me coming from you,' Amora said.

'Hey! I'm right there,' Emma said, pushing Kip out of the frame. Kip didn't even budge.

'You know how much your opinion means to me, Emma. We wouldn't be where we are if you didn't take a risk on me.'

'She's right, you know,' Kip whispered meaningfully into Emma's ear, sounding like he meant something else other than books.

Emma looked to Kip. 'Did you know our authors were making bets on us hooking up?'

'I know. I learnt very recently that having a less tyrannical relationship with our authors is conducive to the editing process. My own authors have been giving me dating advice,' Kip said, grinning. 'You won, didn't you, Amora?'

Emma gasped, slapping his arm. 'You knew!'

'I had a lot riding on it,' Kip said, staring deeply into Emma's eyes with an expression like he was seeing her this way for the first time

'I should leave you two love birds alone now,' Amora said, giggling on the screen and closing the video call before either of them could protest.

Emma turned to Kip. 'What did you bet on?'

'Does it matter?' Kip said, pulling her up.

No, it didn't, Emma thought, taking his hand. 'Where are we going? Where's our food?'

'They're still cooking it.' He intertwined their hands. 'Let's go for a walk by the beach?'

She let him lead her wherever he wanted them to go, grinning and so very in love with him. She took off her white crochet kaftan dress, revealing the purple two-piece swimsuit underneath, and ran to the waters, the coming sunlight giving the blue ocean a silver glimmer. He ran after her, laughing and splashing as he caught her by the waist from behind, their bodies submerged in water.

'I love you, Emma,' he said into her ear, barely a whisper, barely a secret that was unwilling to be kept secret any more. 'I love you,' he said again, louder, as if the second time could make it more true, more sincere, more.

She turned to face him, the sun creating a corona of light around him, and her stomach fluttered and her breath hitched in her chest. The feeling so overwhelming that she felt tears sting in the back of her eyes. She held him, pulled him as close as she could to her body, and answered, 'I love you, Kip. I love you. I love you. I love you.'

Without a shadow of a doubt. Under the bright white light of day. She loved him.

Chapter 24

The Montage Ends

She rolled over in her own bed come Monday morning. They returned the night before. He'd spent the night in her apartment, jostled and crowded by her three cats at the doorway as they entered. He fell on his behind and she on top of him, both laughing.

An arm reached out to his side of her bed—he had his own side now, the one close to the door so that when he turned to look at her in the morning, the sunlight streaming through the floor-to-ceiling window made a corona of light around her body—and finding it empty, she sat up sharply, inexplicably fearing the worst.

She heard the sizzle of oil in a pan and then saw Kip, with thick glasses and ruffled, bedroom hair, standing over the induction cooker in pyjama pants and a loose, black *The Lord of The Rings* shirt—his own clothes this time. He had been staying over at her place so much that she just gave him a drawer of his own. He looked up from the omelettes and smiled at her, brighter than the morning light. She plopped back into bed, breathing a sigh of relief.

She heard the loud beep of the induction cooker echo in the room and Kip's muffled barefoot steps going towards her desk by the window where he laid down two plates of eggs.

She added this scene to the montage, the memory long enough now to write a full novel.

'Wake up, Emma Elizabeth Morales,' he said with a stern tone that he couldn't sustain, offering a hand to help her up, the three cats prowling under the plates of eggs on the table.

Darcy, Wentworth, and Knightley were still pissed off at her for leaving them alone all weekend with only a neighbour feeding them at night. They seemed to be liking Kip more and more, surely because he was feeding them better food when she wasn't looking.

Kip's newly tan skin glowed in the light coming through the window behind him.

'Come to bed, Rudyard Kipling Alegre,' she said, reaching out a lazy arm to him and then surprising him by pulling him on top of her. He landed on her with a loud 'oof', and she locked him in place with her legs around his waist. 'How are you not tired?' She planted her palms on his nape.

'We have proofs waiting in the office,' Kip said, propping himself up on his elbows so he was not crushing her. 'And we spent an obscene amount of money this weekend that we can't get back if we lose our jobs.'

She rolled her eyes and groaned into the side of his neck. 'I hear Jesse is angling for a promotion. I'm sure she can handle a day without us.'

'Emma!' Kip laughed out loud. She felt it in his throat.

His laugh brought her back to the memory of the second day of their trip, lying on their side facing each other on the sand, each preoccupied with a book. Neither had turned the page in the hour that they stayed there waiting for the sunset, each stealing glances at the other. They turned it into a competition for who could maintain focus on their books the longest. They both knew that they'd lost when their eyes met and they laughed out loud at how easy it was for them to fall into schoolyard games to get the other's attention.

Kip pulled her back to the present with a long, tender kiss. 'The eggs will get cold.'

She pouted at him, staring into his eyes pleading for more of . . . this, him. 'Don't you want me?'

He laughed again. 'I thought you just wanted to sleep in— not sleep with me.'

'Both have the word "sleep" in them. To-may-toe, to-mah-toe,' she said, beginning to grind under him.

'Uh-huh . . . Didn't you just say you were tired?' Kip said, the underlying implication being that they'd had so much sex this weekend that it was a miracle they had the energy and stamina to drive back home.

'No, I said, "How are you not tired?" Keep up, Hobbit. We can tell the office we just got back at noon,' she said against his lip, hand going inside his pants. 'Traffic and all that.'

He buried his face in her neck and moaned from the way she was fondling him. 'Sounds about right,' he said airily, taking off their clothes.

Three hours later, they were walking hand and hand to the office—a sharp contrast to that time Kip had walked her from the office to her apartment and waited till she was safely inside before going home. This time, he exited the building with her.

He looked at her, face glowing somehow in the afternoon light, mouthing 'I love you' as if the words were new to both of them.

She grinned back at him, a silly idea coming to her, and she answered him with an 'I know.'

Kip frowned and stopped walking abruptly, dragging her to him. 'Okay, Han Solo, now say the words.'

Emma giggled, wrapping her arms around his waist and shaking her head. 'Of course, I love you. Did you have any doubts, Princess Leia?'

He didn't answer. Instead, he embraced her back, resting his chin on top of her head. 'Always say it back to me, just in case.'

When she nodded, he continued walking again, his hand intertwined in hers.

She sensed trouble when she saw Janey waiting for them in the ground floor lobby. 'Emma! I've been trying to call you all morning!' She turned to Kip. 'Both of you!'

'What happened, Janey?' Emma took out her phone and realized she hadn't opened it since last night. The messages and notifications came pouring in. Her insides turned cold when one notification showed Nick liking the photo she'd posted of her and Kip.

Kip did the same with his phone, but he kept watch of Emma, his face unreadable, save for the wrinkle between his brows.

'It's Nick. He's on our floor waiting for you—with a bouquet of red roses,' Janey said, blocking their way to the elevators.

Emma met Kip's eyes to give him a reassuring look, but whatever expression it was that passed over her face, it seemed to have troubled him more than it reassured. She reached for his hand again and held it tight. She felt his reluctance there, as if the wall that they'd torn down these past days had risen up again between them.

And as if things weren't bad enough, the elevator doors opened and out walked Nick in a leather jacket, holding a bouquet of red roses.

Kip's gaze went to their intertwined hands, which she realized she was holding in a vice-like grip. He moved to let her go. She didn't let him, hoping that her eyes would tell him that he wasn't her second choice.

Janey attempted to stand between them. 'Nick, I told you to go home.'

'Emma can speak for herself,' Nick said, looking past Janey to look at Emma. Emma averted her eyes from him. Kip kept implacably quiet, waiting for what Emma was going to do.

'Make trouble and I call security on you,' Janey said, imposing herself more firmly this time.

'Let me talk to her, Janey.' Nick's gaze dropped to Emma and Kip's intertwined hands.

'Stop, Nick. Go away. Just please go away,' Emma pleaded, tears falling down her cheeks.

Like a splash of cold water to his face, Kip's grip on her hand tightened and he shielded her with his massive body when Nick made to grab her arm. 'Touch her again, and I'll kill you.'

'Is he your rebound?' Nick ignored Kip, looking over his shoulder to meet Emma's gaze. 'Is he why we can't get back together yet? Are you so afraid to be alone that you let just any guy fuck you? I'm here again. I've always been here for you, Emma. Why choose someone new over someone who knows you so much better?'

'If you really knew me, you would have seen that we've been drifting apart for months. It's been over even before I broke up with you.'

'But you kept me around even after you started flirting with *bro* here.' He looked to Kip, who clenched his jaw. 'Alegre, that's your name, right? You had fun on that beach trip? Did she tell you that we go to the beach every year for our anniversary? You never stood a chance against me, Alegre. Emma and I have too much history for her to let go of us so easily. You were just the second choice.'

That seemed to have broken a dam inside Kip, one that held every insecurity he had about being second at everything—second choice for a lover, second choice for the name, second son, second place in a stupid company sports competition. While Kip and Emma were building a history of their love, Nick just showed him his book, thick and dense and solid—seemingly more solid than what she had with Kip.

'Don't listen to him, Kip,' Emma said, holding his hand there as if that was enough to keep him there with her.

Kip frowned and eyed her incredulously. He just stood there as if working up the nerve to say something, to ask the questions behind his eyes.

He shook his head and moved to walk away, his hand slipping from her grasp.

'No, Kip! Don't go!' Emma grabbed his arm to keep him there.

He turned to her with a melancholic look in his eyes, begging her wordlessly to let him go.

It was in that look that she saw that she wasn't the problem here. That there was nothing she could do to quell Kip's doubts about her, about her capacity to break his heart. There was nothing she could do but let him go. So, with a heavy heart and relentless tears, she did.

'That's right, *bro*. Walk away,' Nick said, approaching Emma to drape an arm over her shoulder. Emma tried to push him away, but he held her so tightly, she knew she'd have purple bruises on her skin where Nick's hand had been.

Kip raised a fist at Nick's face, and for a second, Emma thought he was really going to punch Nick. But Kip being Kip, he let out a breath, put down his fist, and backed off.

'I . . . need to think,' Kip said, seeing the way Nick had casually held Emma like he owned her, and backed away from the scene. He was never the kind to fight losing battles, but Emma knew better. Kip was not the kind to bet his whole heart if there was even the slightest chance of him losing. He'd done that once and he lost.

Emma's heart sank, her shoulders slumped as she watched Kip walk away from her. She shrugged Nick off and slapped him. 'No, you walk away, Nick!'

That slap was enough to wipe off the smug look on his face. The betrayed look on his face directed at Emma was enough to remind her of the times Nick had acted like this, like he owned Emma rather than loved her, like it was well within his right to emotionally manipulate her whenever she displeased him, like she shouldn't be acting out like this because she never did act out against Nick even if he did something to displease her when they were together. It had been a long time since they'd broken up, but the look of murder on his face was enough to send Emma spiralling, frozen on the spot, afraid to make any sudden moves and risk angering him more.

Fortunately, Janey was there by her side, blocking Emma from his reach. 'You've humiliated yourself enough. Leave now, or we'll press charges.'

Nick's jaw tensed as he switched glances between Janey and Emma. His gaze settled on Emma, pleading for her to take him back, to not let him walk away the way she did Kip. Emma glared at him. 'I never want to see you again.'

Nick looked like he had been slapped again, startled back and surprised by Emma's sudden distance. 'Don't say that, Emma. I love you.'

'No, you don't. If you had any love for me at all, you would have set me free when I asked.' She swallowed the lump in her throat, wiping the tears from her cheeks and avoiding his eyes. 'I *never* want to see you again.'

Janey took Emma by the arm and ushered her back up to her apartment, leaving behind Nick frozen in time, watching them helplessly as the last chapter of their life together disintegrated by his own hand.

But it had always been clear to Emma where she was now, what story her life had taken. It wasn't her who had any doubts to figure out.

Chapter 25

Dead Flowers

Nick's red roses died a slow, painful death on her kitchen counter over a week after their confrontation. She didn't even remember taking them home, and she hadn't wanted to touch them since she first saw them.

Kip had been lukewarm around her since then and was walking on eggshells around her like she'd proven a point he'd been reluctant to believe until now. She chased after Kip all the way to the parking lot, but he had already gotten into his car when she caught up to him, and he was driving off.

She remembered a thing Kip had said about giving flowers to a lover. *I never liked giving bouquets of flowers. You pluck a flower from the stem, it begins to die. I can't imagine a more aggressive message to send to a lover other than "I love you so much, I'd rather you die in my arms than live without me."*

Life went on like Emma's world wasn't shattering. Work went on like Kip had never once told her he loved her.

They still had book quotas to fill, bills to pay, cats to feed, separate lives to live. Kip spent less and less time in the office while she went to work every day hoping to catch him. When she did catch him in the office, he spent most of his time in Brent's office talking in low voices like they were hatching some great big escape plan.

Now that book fair season was over, they had a short reprieve from the grind right before the holiday shopping season. The editorial team usually took this time to acquire manuscripts for next year, initiate the editing process for pending books, and finalize production for the last few books of the year. The company was very close to reaching the targets that would buy them another year, and Brent predicted that Amora Romero's book would push them to at least break even.

This was how she got Kip to meet with her. Amora had sent the last revised draft of *Menagerie*, which Kip and Emma had to give one last pass before sending for proofreading and layout and design. This was the unpleasant part of book production. Everyone was chasing the deadline, eager to get this book over and done with as soon as possible so they could move on to a new book. This was the part where other departments got involved in the process. And it got particularly messy when the books were by bestselling authors like Amora Romero.

Emma invited him over to her place, unwilling to subject the office to their awkwardness—and to fuel gossip. He declined and picked the place instead, a cozy coffee shop within the suburbs near the office with odd-shaped and colourful flea market furniture, old-school coffee grinders whirring at the counter, and the smell of fresh handmade bread baking in the back room. They agreed to meet there after work hours on a Friday night.

Kip was already waiting for her at a table in the middle of the crowded store. Every other table was occupied by people talking, laughing, drinking, and generally making conversation with each other, completely oblivious to Kip's and Emma's galaxies meeting again. She considered for a moment to cancel and was about to text him when he looked up from his tablet and saw her standing at the doorway. Emma was thankful for the noise because it drowned out just how awkward she felt the moment Kip met her eyes.

He waved at her casually as if that same hand had not woven its way through her hair, hadn't chartered her body like a voyager at sea. She walked up to him, smiling and pretending that seeing him like this didn't pull taut the knots in her stomach. She sat on the chair across from him and took out her laptop, mulling in her head if she should make small talk or ask about his day, how he'd been, if he still loved her.

But this was Work-Kip she was dealing with, and he went right down to work enumerating to her what he thought of the revised manuscript and engaging her in discourse about what to expect from audiences based on the responses from the beta readers. They fell easily into a familiar rhythm. Books had always been their refuge from the world, and it was ironic or poetic or maybe both that they found reprieve from the people they loved together in a thing they loved. They spent the better part of three hours making final annotations to the manuscript that, though not perfect, both agreed was the best version of the story they could come up with in collaboration with the author. After all, that was the job of the book editor. That was to take a raw manuscript, chip at its body in search of the story within, and polish the form that took shape in the aftermath. At the end of the day, all the work was still done by the author.

At midnight, they looked at each other, knowing that they'd done all they could for Amora and sent the manuscript to the next stages of the book production process.

This meant that they did not have the *Menagerie* manuscript to occupy their minds. It was just the two of them now in the middle of a slowly emptying café. Emma moved to pack up her things, but seeing that Kip wasn't doing the same, she stopped, suddenly so very aware of her idle hands. She looked around the room, stealing sidelong glances at Kip who was staring at her from across the table, waiting, just waiting.

People were beginning to leave the place and the barista was beginning to clean up the empty tables. The coffee-grinding machine had been turned off and the oven was already cooling for the night. It reminded her of a scene in romantic comedies like *You've Got Mail*. She felt the pull of a smile on the corners of her lips and thought immediately that it would make him smile, probably even laugh as he was drinking coffee that had gone cold.

'We're in the middle of a trope again.' The words were out of her mouth before she realized it.

Kip straightened up in his seat, eyeing Emma curiously, cautiously. 'What?'

'It's a restaurant . . . Dates, confessions and—' She cleared her throat, realizing too late that the next words coming out of her mouth were stupid. '—breakups. Never mind.'

Save for the wrinkle appearing between his brows, his face was so unreadable that Emma wished that he would just yell at her to get it over with. Instead, he drummed his fingers on the table, mimicking anxious typing on a keyboard as if he were chasing to put words on paper before they disappeared forever in his mind.

'Is that what we're doing here?' Kip finally said, tone flat, hurt and regret behind his eyes that slowly burnt out into a repressed rage. 'You're breaking up with me in the middle of a coffee shop? Like in a romance comedy?' He scoffed.

The way he emphasized 'you' insinuated that he blamed her, that he expected her to be judge, jury, and executioner in a crime neither of them had committed. And it angered her that he would take up such a tone with her. 'Are we? You tell me, Kip. You're the one who's been avoiding me all week.'

It was a stupid idea bringing this up in a public place. It wasn't only stupid; it was cruel and cowardly. It denied either of them the chance to speak their minds, to bear their hearts. It denied them the right to express and discuss their feelings openly. So though both felt anger bubbling in the pit of their stomachs, they kept their tones flat and hushed and charged with words they could not speak, much less scream, out loud.

'I don't want to be the second choice again, Emma. Not with you. I don't know if I could take it if you choose him over me.' He looked away from her, watching the barista clean a table close to the counter as two more customers, a couple who looked young enough to be college students, left the establishment.

Emma clenched her hands into fists on the table. 'I don't know what to tell you for you to believe me that it's you I want, Kip. Tell me what you need me to say. Because apparently "I love you" isn't cutting it.'

'I don't know,' he said. 'What does Nick have to do for you to believe him?'

At this, she felt a spark of lightning crackle in her veins, and she had to lean forward so she could hiss between clenched teeth, 'What does he have to do with any of this?'

'Everything,' Kip said, finally meeting her eyes. 'He said it himself. You have history with him. I never stood a chance.' He shook his head, the drumming had stopped, his Adam's apple bobbed as he swallowed a lump in his throat, and the crease was gone, replaced by softness, a look of defeat that she's never before seen on him. It broke her heart. 'What you feel now? Why you can't get yourself to believe him? I feel the same way. For you.'

She leaned back into her chair, and eyes downcast, quietly, she said, 'So, there's nothing I can tell you for you to believe me?'

'You're not over your ex that's why you keep letting him back into your life.'

The implication being that he wasn't over his own ex.

She made all the arguments in her head. Love was opening gates, letting in a person apart from oneself, hoping they'd fill the space of her empty rooms, and trusting them not to break her house. She'd bared her heart, body, mind, and soul to him, and opened herself up to him in a way she'd never done for anyone, not even Nick. She let herself be defenceless with him for what was the point of love if not showing both the good and bad parts, both the impregnable and vulnerable parts? Once we loved someone, we could never really unlove them, could never really take away the rooms they inhabit, only dictate the spaces where they were allowed to occupy. There was really no going back once we opened the gates to someone else. They'd have left their marks inside.

It was why she thought Kip was brilliant not to close his own gates to his ex and instead let her in where she could not break him again. Thieves broke into a house, stole valuables, and left in the night. Guests visited in the light of day, brought gifts, and left with promises of returning as friends. He was still friends with his ex. He'd be a hypocrite to stop her from doing the same.

An epiphany dawned on her, one that she should have realized because she felt it too. It was the same reason she couldn't let Nick back in. It was why history with their exes held so much more power over them. Her history with Nick was a proven track record of her breaking hearts. Kip's history with his ex was the foundation of a life he could have had.

They were both afraid of what the other could do to hurt them.

'No, Kip,' she said finally, beginning to pack her bag just so she was doing something with her hands. 'This isn't about me and Nick at all. It's about you.'

'Me? How is this about me?'

'You don't trust me. Because I've broken someone else's heart, you're afraid I'm capable of doing it again. Because you're afraid to risk losing a future you want again, you're choosing not to make plans at all with anyone, not just me.'

'How do I trust you when you have so much history with him? How do I trust that you're not repeating history with me? That I'm not just some rebound to cover up the fact that you're not over him?'

'That book's closed—forever!' she said a little louder than intended, drawing the attention of the barista and the last few customers. She took in a deep breath and then another to calm herself down. 'That story is over.' She faced him and levelled him with a gaze that she hoped showed what he was becoming, what he was doing, what he was unconsciously choosing. 'The difference between you and Nick? I broke his heart when I let myself fall out of love with him, but I chose to stop breaking his heart by setting him free. You? I haven't broken your heart yet, but you're breaking mine—you're choosing to break mine.'

She stood up and hooked the sling of her bag over her shoulder. She waited for him to say something, but he didn't. He turned away, his fist trembling on the table, the wrinkle returning, his eyes misting over. 'I wish you'd stay long enough to see this through the end, Kip. You'll see no one was even close. No one but you.'

And she left him there, feeling like a rose plucked from the stem and wondering if he felt the same way.

Chapter 26

Greatest Fears

Fear was the suspension of good things in anticipation for the bad. It was a prolonged tension that demanded release.

A good jump scare usually did that trick for most people, which was what Emma had intended to give herself by going on a Stephen King movie marathon on Halloween day.

No dice. Her mind kept wandering off to thoughts and feelings she'd been trying to suppress since she'd last seen Kip—thoughts and feelings that were far scarier than any Stephen King story.

Janey, meanwhile, lay on her bed engrossed by gore after gore, weird after weird, through *Pet Sematary*, *Children of The Corn*, *Cujo*, and *Gerald's Game*. Now they were watching *Misery*. They had been at it since the crack of dawn, living in what felt like a semi-catatonic state and moving from their position only to go to the bathroom or get their food delivery at the door. Darcy, Knightley, and Wentworth were lying next to Emma on a foldable mattress on the floor next to Janey's bed. Several bottles of wine, bags of Halloween candies, and all manner of junk food littered the room. Emma's cats were eyeing the tub of half-full melted vanilla ice cream on the floor within Emma's reach. Janey and Emma were wearing Halloween-themed sleeping clothes that Janey insisted on so she could post stories on Instagram to get her current paramour's attention.

Emma and her cats had been staying at Janey's apartment, knowing that Nick would try to reach her at hers. Nick was still trying to contact her through Janey, asking to meet up and talk. She'd ignored all his messages and had even gone to a lawyer to get a restraining order against Nick.

Brent had given the rest of the company the Halloween weekend while accounting was drawing up the numbers and making forecasts on how much they could stand to still earn before the end of the year. More importantly, they were determining if their efforts had bought them another year of operations. They wouldn't know till next week if they still had jobs next year, so most of the editorial department had filed for longer vacation leaves at the end of December.

Emma had actually planned this movie marathon for Kip in anticipation of that big announcement, knowing that they'd try to out-nerd the other as they watched, distracting themselves from the scary, real-world news with scary, made-up stories.

It was the oldest trick in the book. The main character watched a scary movie with their love interest and voila! A convenient, surefire way to orchestrate moments of intimacy and vulnerability between characters.

Emma's intention was to make him laugh and add to the 'two nerds standing in the middle of a nerdy joke' thing they had going on. She had made it her life goal to make him laugh at least once a day. She hadn't heard his laugh in weeks.

'My one caveat with this story is Paul Sheldon being a "romance novelist"—' Emma did air quotes, '—when Misery Chastain dies in his book.' She turned to look at Kip and was disappointed when it was Janey who looked back at her from atop the bed, popcorn halfway to her mouth. Emma had been so engrossed with her thoughts that for a moment she'd forgotten where she was. She was expecting Kip to answer with something silly like 'You know Annie Wilkes is doing for Paul Sheldon what we do for authors—minus the feet cutting part.' And she would answer, 'Did you just compare our jobs to the personification of cocaine?' She had already imagined how loud he would have laughed.

Janey eyed her with the intensity of an intermediate reader going through a Russian novel. She tapped the space bar of her laptop sitting between them, pausing the movie projected on the wall opposite Janey's bed. 'You forgot again that it's me you're with, Ems.'

'Sorry. I was just in my head too much,' Emma said, reaching for the space bar of the laptop.

Janey slapped her hand away. 'I don't want to watch this movie any more. It's too on the money for both of us.'

'We can watch something else. What about *Carrie*?' she said, scrolling through the movies saved on her laptop.

'Don't want a reminder of my PMS,' Janey answered.

'*The Dome*?'

'Not Halloween enough.'

'*The Dead Zone*?'

'Too political.'

'*It*?'

'Clowns scare the bejeezus out of me,' Janey said, shutting the laptop abruptly and barely missing Emma's fingers. 'Why don't we just talk about our love lives?'

'Took you long enough!' Emma scooched up close to Janey and bounced up and down on the bed. Janey had been dodgy about her dating life lately, which was totally out of character for her as Janey wasn't the kind to skirt around sensitive topics, choosing instead to deal with them with the straightforwardness—and utter brazenness—of a wrecking ball. The devil was in the details for Janey and she was never afraid to confront him, to put emphasis on him the way an editor with a red pen would encircle a major plot loophole in a manuscript. Not until now. 'I really thought you were going to keep it in for the rest of your life. Spill!'

Janey scowled at her, sensing immediately Emma's ulterior motive. 'Just because I'm heartbroken doesn't mean I need you to pretend that you're okay for me, got it, Ems? I would be happier if we were both miserable at the same time together.'

Emma groaned and sidled closer to Janey, leaning back into the headboard. Even when she was dealing with heartbreak, Janey was still the frenetic ball of energy that people knew her to be. She only let herself be vulnerable around Emma. 'You have an odd definition for happiness, Janey.'

She shrugged. 'Misery loves company.'

Emma leaned on Janey's shoulder. 'Enough dilly-dallying, Flores. Talk! What really happened between you and Theo after that first date? You were so into him that it's hard for me to believe that you'd just give up on him like that. You're not the kind who backs down from a fight. Is it because of this new mysterious man you're seeing?'

Janey was also the kind who denied love every waking moment of her life and yet got swept up by it so easily when it came. In everything else, Janey was steadfast, so sure and so protective of who she was and the life she was building for herself. And yet when she fell in love, everything else fell to the wayside.

'Doesn't matter who the other guy is. He was just my rebound. Theo and I met again two weeks ago—' she held up a hand just as Emma was about to comment, '—as friends!'

Emma pulled away from Janey to stare impatiently at her. 'Aaand?'

'I ended up going to his house and—' she covered her face with her hands, muffling the next words out of her mouth, '—staying the night!'

Emma gasped. 'Did you—'

'God, no! We just talked all night. It was the sweetest thing really. There was no sex, but it was the closest I've ever felt with another human.' She put down her hands and looked up at the wall, the projector still flashing Annie Wilkes holding a mallet on the ceiling. 'The first time we dated we couldn't really connect so I ghosted him after sex, and I started seeing another guy—someone hotter and better in bed, I might add, but after that, when the sex became less and less interesting, nothing. He ghosted me! Me? Would you believe it?'

'Janey, know that I'm saying this as a friend, but you kind of had it coming. I'm not saying you deserve it, but ghosting people is just cruel and juvenile.'

Janey rolled her eyes. 'Well, I know that now, Ems! So, I texted Theo to apologize. He asked to meet—as friends!—and we just clicked. We've been seeing and messaging each other regularly since.'

'So, what's the problem? Date him!'

Janey took too long to answer. It was only when Emma was looking her in the eye trying to guess what was bothering her did Janey confess. 'He has a girlfriend.'

'Janey!' Emma slapped her friend's arm but she didn't move away.

'Emma!' This time it was Janey leaning on Emma's shoulder for support.

'How could you?' Emma finally said, after considering what to say to her friend. How could someone so close to her heart do something as crass and cruel as this to another girl?

'I know,' Janey said, sighing. 'I know. I'm a miserable, cruel bitch. I missed my chance because I gave up on the first try. He met her after I ghosted him! I'm the dumb bitch who couldn't see what was good if it was standing in front of her, and now I'm trying to take it away from another girl.'

Janey wasn't a bad person. She wasn't a good person either. She wasn't perfect, but Emma knew Janey, and no one knew Emma that way Janey knew her. People were complicated creatures, and people falling in love was a powder keg waiting to explode at any moment of friction. Love couldn't be contained, couldn't be controlled, but it couldn't have been done alone. Not if they turned into Annie Wilkes.

Love was the thing that healed a broken heart. Love was the thing that finally let Emma let go of the past. Love was why Emma was truly and completely letting go of Nick, even if no new love was waiting for her after. And she was fine being alone because she wasn't alone. She loved Janey. She loved her cats. She loved her books. She loved herself first.

'You're too harsh on yourself, Janey.' Emma held Janey's hand, and Janey squeezed back. 'You couldn't have done it alone anyway. What matters is that you and Theo do what's fair for the other girl if you two are sure about doing this.'

'You talk like you know what you're talking about,' Janey said with an effort to invoke humour, but it fell flat. 'Typical for the romance editor to know love, I guess.'

'That is not factual, Janey. I don't know what I'm doing when it's about matters of the heart.'

'That's true. I know for a fact that you had to be pushed into a mosh pit before you date a guy—or forced into working with another to get over the first one.' They both laughed at that.

'"The only true wisdom is knowing you know nothing." If there's one thing I don't know much about, it's love. I could read a thousand love stories and never truly understand what it is. I could make assumptions, guesses, and wild theories, but when it's standing right there in front of me, I wouldn't know what to do with it. Do I embrace it? Do I push it away? Do I hit it with a stick?'

Janey gave her a conspiratorial grin, the one she made when she thought of something insane—and probably lewd. Most likely lewd. 'Oh! So that's what you're doing wrong.'

'I'm being serious here, Janey!'

'Seriously, "hit that" doesn't mean hit him with a stick. See, Janey knows a thing or two about love.'

Emma cast Janey a mischievous sidelong glance, and she grinned. 'But I did hit that, Janey.'

Janey shrieked and then laughed so loud she startled Emma's cats. 'Well, look at you.'

'But seriously, Janey. Will you be okay? Are you ready to face the consequences of your love?'

Janey nodded. 'I think I'll be fine. I made my bed; now, I'll lie in it.' They stayed like that, staring at Annie Wilkes with a mallet on the wall like it was a reflection of their worst selves coming to life. 'I'm sorry it didn't work out with Kip though,' Janey said after a long silence. 'I guess he was just too heartbroken from his last relationship to give his heart so easily to you.'

'What do you mean? Kip and his ex are friends. He's *ninong* to her child.'

'Really? Lily asked Kip to be *ninong* to her child? That's just . . . cruel of her.'

Emma turned her head sharply to face Janey. 'You knew his ex?'

'Knew her? I worked with her. She was the editor you replaced. Remember Lily?'

She sat up straight. 'No! Lily interviewed me for the job!'

'Kip never mentioned it to you?' Janey sat up straight, too, eyeing Emma curiously. 'Her husband is Brent. Lily and Brent dated a million years ago. In college, I think.'

'But Brent is Kip's best friend . . . '

She paused, thinking, even though Janey wasn't really expecting an answer. 'Hey! So, history does matter. Kip just chose between his ex and his best friend. Is that why he's leaving for New Zealand next month?'

'What? How did you know that?'

'I was gossiping with HR about who's resigning before and after the big announcement. Apparently, Kip has been asking about taking a long sabbatical from the company to think about his options.'

'What?' Emma stood from the bed and scrambled for her phone somewhere on the floor.

'Girl, what's happening?' Janey scooched over to the edge of the bed. 'You look like you've seen a ghost.'

'I'm . . . I'm just . . . I'm scared.' She tilted her head up, her mind swirling with questions and doubts and every word she'd exchanged with Kip since the start of the year and ended up staring at Annie Wilkes and her mallet. What were they doing dicking around like they had all the time in the world? What was she doing letting the past dictate what the future held? 'I'm terrified that I'm about to lose him forever.'

Chapter 27

The Backstory

The first samples of *Menagerie* came on the day of the publishing house's Christmas party. It was a modest affair, made more special by the prize money they'd won from the corporate sports fest, which allowed them to bring in family and friends. So, the open office setup was more crowded today than usual.

Brent called her into his office to see the *Menagerie* samples. Pride welled up inside like hot chocolate foam as she held the book in her hands. It was a year's worth of work, but holding the book now just washed away any agony she had felt in that time. In fact, she was tearing up a little bit.

'I remember that feeling,' a woman sitting on the couch behind her said, making Emma turn around sharply. She recognized the woman as the editor who'd interviewed her for the job so many years ago. She had resigned a month after Emma started. Lily continued, 'Seeing a book you've been working on for so long it begins to feel like it's never going to get done. And then it gets done, and there's the book in your hand.'

Lily was holding her sleeping baby in her arms, cooing and rocking it slightly. She smiled at Emma, and it was like staring at the sun on a bright, beautiful day. It was no wonder that her shadow over Kip's heart was so long and overpowering.

'Lily! It's been so long since I last saw you!'

'It's so good to see you thriving in this company, Emma. I hope you decide to stay.'

'That was my news to tell, Lily,' Brent said without the hint of derision that the words implied. Emma turned back too sharply towards Brent that she thought she felt whiplash. There was only devotion for the woman in his eyes, only pure, unadulterated love for his wife and child.

'What are you talking about? Am I fired? Is the company closing?'

'No!' Brent said, pausing as if to consider how to better explain his point. 'We almost closed down, but we got a bid from an international publisher for the international distribution of this book. It gave us the boost we needed to go above and beyond the required sales target. So, for now, we're safe.' Brent stood up from his desk and walked around towards her so that he could sit on the edge of his table. 'Once we get back on our feet and regain Corporate's confidence in us, I'd like to promote you to managing editor. I want you to start up a new romance fantasy imprint and grow it. You've got good instincts. We need that to carry us over into the years to come.'

'But what about Kip?'

Brent and Lily exchanged looks. 'What about him?' Brent asked.

'Janey said he's leaving because the company is closing.'

Brent sighed, and Lily laughed. 'I told you, Janey is the source of all gossip circulating in this office,' Lily said.

'Unfortunately, not all of it is accurate or true for that matter,' Brent said, pressing the bridge of his nose with his thumb and index finger. 'I haven't made the announcement yet, so try not to tell Janey about this till I get to say it, okay?'

'What about Kip?' Emma insisted. She hadn't seen him in a while, and she'd been texting him, messaging him, making calls, but he wouldn't answer any of them. Did he hate her so much that he would block her out of his life completely? She began to cry again, this time, miserable ugly-cry tears. 'He isn't talking to me any more, and I don't know how to fix it.' She stared accusingly at them both. 'And it's because of you two. How could you do that to Kip? How could you make him *ninong* after you broke up with him?'

'Emma, he broke up with me,' Lily said, standing up, baby in her arms.

Emma gasped.

'It was a kindness that neither of us deserved,' Brent said. 'I really did try to stay away.'

'I was falling back in love with Brent, but I wanted to keep fighting for our relationship, for Kip. Because of course I wanted to keep fighting for him. We have history,' Lily added. 'Kip saw that it was making everyone miserable. So, one day, he just came up to us and said, "I yield. You and Brent are more important to me, Lily." And that was that.'

'I have to say this, Emma,' Brent added, joining their little huddle. 'I've never seen Kip as happy as he has been these past months with you, and he's an idiot for not seeing that.'

'He said he's flying to New Zealand tonight, didn't he?' Lily said, looking to Brent for confirmation, but instead got a raised eyebrow.

'So, he *is* leaving?' Emma said, her mind going blank. Kip was actually leaving.

Lily nudged her, 'You should go after him before it's too late.'

Brent opened his mouth to talk but got a glare from his wife instead. 'He should be at the airport now. You can still catch him.' He took his car keys from his pocket, looking at Lily like he was waiting for approval (she nodded) before he handed Emma the keys. 'Take our car.'

They prodded her out the door, and she was too surprised and confused not to protest.

Before she left, she caught glimpses of conversation between husband and wife.

'Who's going to get the car at the airport?' Brent asked.

'You. The car was your idea,' Lily said. 'Get me my phone. We can still give them a romance-worthy happily-ever-after.'

'Ay, romance editors!' Brent said, bemused, endearing.

Chapter 28

A Romance Fantasy Ending

Emma was back in the parking lot of the airport, a potted cactus sitting on the passenger seat next to her. And like that first time, that first lesson of romance, she was beginning to see that this was such a stupid plan. She didn't know what time his flight was or which aeroplane he was boarding. She just knew what Brent and Lily had told her.

It was December, and the airport was crowded with people transiting to and from everywhere. She convinced herself that she'd stay here and watch every plane bound for New Zealand take flight from the tarmac. There weren't that many. The holiday season was lending a euphoric mood to the airport, as if the nexus between a million places, the interim where goodbyes and hellos were exchanged, was an inherently happy place, wasn't the setting for many breakups and reunions in love stories. The asphalt grey shone with silver specks. The metal and glass fixtures glittered in afternoon daylight and nightlights. And the curved stone structure towering over the parking lot was merely the gateway to the world and skies and beyond. Everything here seemed larger than life. Everything here was leaving for someplace else. Everything here seemed happier, more jubilant than anywhere else, and Emma felt out of place sitting in a borrowed car with a cactus and a phone sitting unnervingly still on the passenger seat.

Janey had been messaging her every few minutes demanding updates. The last message was Janey asking her where she was. Emma had replied with 'parking lot'. Her best friend messaged again, 'Which parking lot specifically?'

When Emma gave her her exact location, Janey replied with a cryptic 'Stay there.'

Another message came from the last person she wanted to hear from now.

'I'm sorry, Emma—N,' Nick said in his message, using a new number!

She had thrown her phone on the passenger seat next to the cactus and waited and waited and waited. That was hours ago. As if she had nowhere else to go to but home and that felt too much like giving up, like defeat. And she wasn't ready to admit that yet, not even when she didn't have any moves left—at least not anything sensible. She could do a *Love Actually* and risk getting arrested as she tried to run past every security block on the way to the boarding area. Actually, it wasn't just a risk. She would for sure get arrested if she tried that. If she was desperate enough, she could blow all her savings and buy a ticket to New Zealand—and never get on the plane because she didn't have the visa to go to the country. This plan was becoming dumber and dumber as she thought about it.

She would cringe at the dumb idea, but instead she smiled. It would be the ultimate punchline to their long-running 'two nerds standing in the middle of nerdy joke,' her chasing after her lover in the airport hoping to stop him before he left her forever. She pressed her forehead on the wheel and sighed.

She hit her forehead lightly on the wheel as the thoughts came barrelling in her mind. Maybe she did mess it all up. *Thump.* Maybe she did lose Kip. *Thump. Thump.* Maybe Kip was never hers to lose. *Thump. Thump. Thump.*

Her thoughts spiralled till she reached a point where she was convincing herself to just admit defeat and go home. She wasn't the problem here. She was sure she loved him. She had never been more sure. It was Kip who wouldn't believe her.

Her phone rang, vibrating against the orange clay pot of the small golden barrel cactus she'd impulsively bought for Kip on the way here. This was the most expensive cactus they had at the store. She thought, as she was choosing what to give Kip— to make the grand romantic gesture because he was secretly romantic and he secretly loved rom-coms—if she was giving him a cactus to send the message that she loved him so much that she wanted to spend her miserable prickly life with him, she might as well give him the fanciest one she could find. She'd mocked him when he said he'd give a girl a potted plant or better yet a cactus instead of dying flowers. Why did she think this was a good idea now? Who thought a cactus was fancy?

She was just absently hitting the wheel with her forehead at this point, her skin beginning to numb. She couldn't stay in the airport parking lot forever. She'd been here all afternoon, and night was beginning to creep in. There was the overnight parking fee and security might arrest her anyway for suspicious behavior. The guard who checked her car on the way in had already thought the cactus was weird. More so the tattered, faded *The Lord of The Rings* shirt she wore over jeans. She had stolen it from Kip's luggage that morning after they returned from the beach. She thought it would be romantic, showing up in one of his nerdy shirts.

Boy, was she failing at this romance thing.

A knock on the driver seat window startled her into hitting the car horn, and she pressed the window button without looking at who it was on the outside.

'Sorry, officer, I'm leaving,' she lied, intending to move to a different parking spot and looking up to smile at the guard only to find that it wasn't security at all.

It was Kip, holding a bouquet of red roses.

'I was wrong about the roses. It's the other way around,' he said, breathless like he'd run a marathon.

'What?' Emma answered, jaw dropped, brows knitted together.

He pulled open the car door and offered a hand to her to help her out. She accepted his hand, suddenly feeling underdressed next to him in a white button down shirt with the sleeves folded up to his elbows, beige khakis the colour of yellowing book pages, square, black-rimmed glasses, and dark brown loafers. He steadied her as she stood, placing one hand on her waist as the other held the roses up between them. 'The flowers, they're not telling you that I would rather you die in my arms than live without me—' He stopped, looking at her from head to toe, brows knitting, eyes flashing in recognition of his shirt. 'What are you wearing, you big nerd?'

'I was trying to be romantic!' she said, burying her face in the crook of his neck.

'Is that why you were waiting for me at the airport? You were going to chase me like that kid in *Love Actually*?'

'I thought it was a good idea when I first thought of it, okay? For a few hours, I thought it was going to be *Casablanca*.'

'You know security *will* arrest you if you even try a *Love Actually*.'

She leaned back to look at his face. 'And thus, I was waiting for you in the parking lot of the airport.'

'So, you just took a chance and came here today of all days to chase me in an airport? How do you even know for sure I was flying to New Zealand tonight?'

'I don't! Brent and Lily told me you'd be here! I thought it was going to be romantic!' She pulled away and dove into the car to get the cactus. 'I even got you a stupid cactus because you said bouquets of flowers basically say "I want you to die."' She held out the pot to him. 'Now, you're giving me roses. You're confusing me, Kip!'

Kip laughed out loud and took her free hand in his. 'I told you I changed my mind. These roses are me telling you, "I love you so much, I cannot imagine life without you."'

'We're not very good at this romance thing, are we?' she said, looking away from him.

'We're just two book nerds standing in the middle of a nerdy joke,' he said, taking the cactus from her and setting it on top of the car with the roses. He then wrapped her arms around his neck and placed his hands on her waist, humming a song and swaying them in a slow dance under the light of the single streetlamp near Janey's car.

'What are we doing, Kip?'

'Dancing like in the romance stories we like. The weatherman said it'll be a rainy night. We'd be hitting two tropes at once.'

Despite herself, she giggled, and he seemed pleased by it. 'What are you talking about, you Hobbit?'

'Your ex, he messaged me. He said, "You win."'

She scowled. 'And you listened to him?'

'Of course not. I told him to go fuck himself. You're a person, not a prize.'

'Then why? What changed your mind? How did you even know that I was here anyway, Kip?'

'I was at home binge-watching Nora Ephron movies and thinking when Brent and Lily called me to say that they sent you here to find me. Before that, your best friend harassed my best friend, who also happens to be our boss, about my love life. Brent and I have been skirting around the topic of my breakup with my ex—his wife—for years. I've been the second choice for so long, I thought that was what I'll always be. So, I stopped trying to take risks. I gave up every fight before I even tried. In fact, I stopped trying at all. When Janey called him about us, Brent forced me to finally confront him about any issues I had left from my past relationship.'

'And what did he tell you?'

'He said I was an idiot for letting you go. He said he has never seen me as happy as I was with you than when I was with Lily. He said, you're nothing like Lily. He said, you're not Lily and not everyone is Lily.'

Emma pulled away from Kip's hold, far enough to look at his face, but not too far that he had to let go of her. 'What did you say?' she asked, staring deep into his intense eyes.

'I said, it was the other way around. Lily isn't you. No one is you. You're the girl of my dreams, Emma. You've been the girl in all my wildest fantasies even before I first saw you reading *The Princess Bride* in the lobby. You're the biggest book nerd I know, probably even bigger than I am. You're so sexy I lose my mind every time you let me touch you. I read every book reference you throw at me after we banter just so I can keep up with you. I've never read so many romance books in my life just so I can impress someone. And you floor me every time you make a sci-fi or fantasy reference. I never stood a chance against you, Buttercup. I'm sorry it took me so long to realize this. I was an idiot to think it was important that I was your second choice. I don't care if I were your second, your third, your fourth, as long as I'm your last, Emma.'

Emma didn't know she was crying until Kip brushed a tear off her cheek with his thumb. 'But aren't you leaving for New Zealand?'

'What are you talking about? My life is here. My job is here. You're here.'

'Job? But Brent said I was getting promoted.'

'He'll be creating a new position for you, Emma. I'm not getting fired. At least not that I know of . . . '

'But your family . . . '

'I'm beginning to think that you actually want me to go to New Zealand,' he said, laughing. 'Just say the word, I'll buy us plane tickets and you can chase me all over the airport all you want.'

'No! I mean, yes! I mean I don't want you to be alone or lonely any more, Kip—' She groaned. 'Fuck! How am I so bad at this? I had a speech prepared and everything!'

Emma knew that she wasn't getting her point across when she saw a frown was beginning to pull his lips downward, but he waited for her to finish.

'You bewitched me, Kip. Body and soul,' Emma blurted out, because Jane Austen always knew what to say. 'You don't need me to be anything else but myself. You don't ask me to break off pieces of my heart, but by just being in my life, you fill up the empty spaces in my heart and soul. You like what I like. You love what I love. You know me so well, sometimes you terrify me when you show me parts of myself that I never knew were there. And you make being so nerdy so sexy. How is that even possible?' His laugh made her feel braver, bolder, more honest, and the words just flowed out of her. 'You're the hero in all my fantasies. You're the jargon in sci-fi that I'm never sure I understand completely, but I still want to try. You're the only love interest I could imagine sharing a romance happy ending with. You're my chosen one, Kip. It could only be you.'

'Even if I'm too tall to be a Hobbit?'

'There's more of you to climb.'

'Even if I'm nothing like leather-clad, swashbuckling Westley?'

'Inigo Montoya was a more interesting character anyway.'

'Even if I get so hot whenever I'm around you that I could burn paper?'

'Then let the world burn. I burn only for you, Hobbit.'

'I love you, Emma.'

'I know,' Emma said, grinning when he frowned, but before he could complain, she followed it up with, 'I love you so much, Kip.'

Kip captured her mouth in a kiss so deep and so loving and so very intimate that no one else could have kissed her the way he did at that moment.

And because two book nerds kissing and dancing in the parking lot far, far away from the airport where most romance stories ended—with a grand gesture or a chase scene before the gates closed—was as far from romantic as it could get, it started to rain hard, drenching their clothes, drowning the cactus and the dying roses on the car, playing a love song on the asphalt, the glass, the steel frames, and the towering stone structure.

The romance gods probably had a sense of humour or maybe they were just hopelessly romantic. Nonetheless, art or science or any sort of supernatural intervention had nothing to do with this moment playing out the way it did. Kip and Emma made their choice, and in their book, their love story was one for the books.

Epilogue

One Year Later

The aftermath of a happy ending can feel anticlimactic. After all, it's just the rest of life carrying on as if an event akin to the big bang hadn't just happened.

It was December again, and Emma and Kip went to New Zealand to celebrate Christmas with his family. Finally!

Christmas with family was one of those things you took for granted until it was gone completely. Emma's mom, her only family until she met Kip, had passed away in the first year of the pandemic, and she'd been celebrating the last three Christmases alone in her apartment with her three cats, while eating fancy, definitely non-Christmas-y takeout food and getting stupid drunk on convenience store booze.

Three months prior, they were in Kip's bed the day after the book fair, and she'd woken up to him, lying on his side and watching her sleep.

'What's up, Humbert Humbert?' she said, her voice still hoarse from sleep.

'You know you can just say you want space,' he said, laughing and moving away from her in his bed. 'And you're more like Dulcinea than Lolita to me, Buttercup.'

'Comparing me to objectified women in literature is really killing the mood for morning sex, Don Quixote.' She pulled him back to her, pressing her face against his chest to listen to his heartbeat. 'Tell me what's on your mind.'

He rolled his eyes in jest. *What man can pretend to know the riddle of a woman's mind?'*

'Not making it any better, Hobbit,' she said into his chest.

'Yes, yes, you are the queen of book references. I yield to you. I need you to get up now.' He pulled her to sit up, so they were sitting side by side and leaning back into the headboard. She groaned in protest the entire time. The position gave them a full unbridled view of Kip's bookshelf and toy collection. He placed a plain white envelope in her palm with the note written on the front: *It's dangerous business, Frodo, going out of your door.'*

'What's this, Gandalf?' Emma asked him, feeling the outside of the envelope to guess what was inside.

'Open it!' he said, buzzing with so much energy, likely pent up from waiting for her to wake up, while he watched her open the envelope. He was barely holding back a laugh.

She pulled out two roundtrip aeroplane tickets bound for New Zealand. She looked up at him, wide-eyed and stunned. 'Kip, this is . . . I can't . . . '

Kip took her hands in his. 'Please say yes? I really want you to meet my family.'

'But this is worth more than a month's salary, Kip!'

'It's already been paid for,' Kip said, beginning to ramble and fidget with her fingers, his bedraggled hair, his glasses, unwilling to give her a chance to argue with him about this. 'I've been saving up for this trip all year. I have some frequent flyer miles. And I got the tickets on sale. Don't worry about the cost. Just worry about your visa.'

Emma looked at the plane tickets in her hand and then at Kip's hopeful, expectant face, and she knew without a shadow of a doubt that she really wanted to go. 'Let me pay you back? I can't obviously do it in one go—'

It was like a light bulb blinked open behind his eyes and a big, joyful smile sliced across his face. 'Does this mean you're saying yes?'

She took her time answering him, hoping to make him sweat a little in anticipation. In the entire year that they'd been dating, Kip still wouldn't make assumptions with Emma. He always gave her the chance to articulate her thoughts and choices. But unlike before when it was fuelled by doubt and fear, this time, it was mutual respect and reassurance that they were each equal participants in their relationship.

'I know you're desperate to prove that I actually live in a Hobbit hole,' he joked to ease his growing tension.

She grinned, and instantly, he relaxed. 'Of course, I want to go with you. Did you have any doubts?'

'Not at all,' he said, grinning, pulling her to him to kiss her. 'The tickets are non-refundable.'

'I did promise you that I'll make your parents love me more than they love you.'

He narrowed his eyes at her and pursed his lips in mock annoyance. 'You know what, I change my mind. You don't need to meet my parents!'

She laughed and straddled him so that she was looking away from the toys. 'Admit it, you just don't want to go to Hobbiton alone.'

He pulled her closer to him by her hips, his hands remaining there as he met her eyes. 'Figured I'd look and feel less like a nerd if I brought my hot girlfriend with me instead of my parents.'

'Kip, it's Hobbiton. Nothing could make it less nerdy,' she said, leaning in to kiss him. 'Besides, nerdy is sexy . . . '

And so here they were, walking hand-in-hand on the dirt path of Hobbiton. Kip's family—three pairs of parents with a gaggle of children—went ahead, following the tour guide who delivered trivia after trivia about the movies, the author, and the books. Emma and Kip fell behind, stopping at every round door they passed on the side of the hill to take photos.

Kip was right about his parents loving her almost as soon as they met her. She had never met anybody who loved books as much as she did, maybe even more, and Kip literally had to save her from his parents who had been talking with her for hours about books the day they landed in the country. Their family home in New Zealand, which she had proven was not in fact a Hobbit hole, had big windows and brick walls. It was light and airy and so open. It felt homey, lived in, and loved in a way that her apartment once felt when her mom was still alive and living with her. The Alegres had even dedicated one room for a home library. Although his brothers had already moved out of their family home to start their own families, the family didn't break apart. In fact, it just grew bigger and closer. And Emma's heart ached knowing that a family like this could exist while she'd only had her mother her entire life.

In fact, all this? Life in general? It all felt so surreal to her, this real-life happily-ever-after, and she sometimes had to pinch herself just to know that this wasn't a dream or worst, a daydream she used to escape to when things got really bad in real life. That she'd have to wake up eventually.

Kip and Emma decided to move in together and were looking for a bigger place near their office that could fit all their books and their pets. She finally had a family again to celebrate the holidays with. Her career practically skyrocketed after the success of *Menagerie*, which birthed a new imprint that she would build up as managing editor.

Of course, life carried on for the rest of the world, too, after Kip and Emma's happily-ever-after.

Amora wrote two more manuscripts, one romance and one fantasy, which Emma and Kip more than happily divided between themselves to work separately on. Brent and Lily had another baby, and this time they'd asked both Kip and Emma to be its *ninong* and *ninang*. Nick had a new girlfriend, a musician like him, and had signed on with a record label company. He and his band were releasing their first album next year. They were not friends any more, but they remained in each other's lives as shards of memories from their shared history. Janey had married Theo last year, just a few months after he'd broken up with his then-girlfriend. It was a whirlwind romance, but that was to be expected from her best friend who had always been this frenetic ball of energy wherever she went.

And Kip? He only became braver, bolder, and less reluctant to take risks. He was no longer afraid to be second best at anything—though Emma could tell that it still displeased him when he lost in something silly like a relay game at the company team-building program. In fact, he was taking bigger leaps in life in general. Kip had written a book and was signed on by a literary agent. His agent had been hinting that there was a three-way bidding match for his Filipino mythology-inspired epic fantasy novel. He had adopted a cat and a dog from the animal shelter. And he was actually the one who had asked Emma to move in with him. Kip had become the orbit around whom she found balance in the world, her guiding north star in the darkest nights, her sun in a universe that felt too vast, too empty for one small life. Kip felt like home, like a Hobbit hole, and that meant comfort.

Which was why, when Kip took her hand and brought her to Bag End, she wasn't surprised when he knelt before her, holding up the one ring to her. He knew her. He saw her. He loved her. She didn't doubt him for one second.

Nor did he doubt her.

In most love stories, this would be the ending, the promise of a lifetime in each other's lives, a vow to love each other so long as they both shall live.

But to Emma, this didn't feel like the end. Not even a beginning. Only a continuation of a lifetime of love and comfort and joy and adventures spent with each other.

Did love ever have an end? Emma supposed not. Someone always had to carry on the story.

The End

Acknowledgments

This book came out of nowhere. When I first wrote it, I wrote it for myself, and I planned to hide it away forever. Maybe it's too much to say that this book in your hand was destiny, as destiny had nothing to do with the work that went into turning my secret story into this book. So many people brought this book out of the shadows and into the light. I could never sufficiently express my gratitude to these people:

Nora Nazarene Abu Bakar, Publisher of Penguin Random House SEA, you were the first to take a chance on me and my stories. I was in the trenches for so long that I almost gave up. But like in love, a story only needs one fated chance to get it right. I will never forget that it was you who gave me that chance.

Thatchaayanie Renganathan, my wonderful, wonderful editor—it was so much fun working with you for my stories. I've never met anyone who really gets what I'm driving at in my writing like you do. Thank you, thank you so much. Here's to working on more books together? (I promise I'll try to stick to my deadlines next time.)

Chaitanya Srivastava, my publicist and a social media genius, you've been so excited for my story even when I find myself doubting everything I create! If it weren't for you, I wouldn't have the coolest encounters with my favorite authors and the crazy endorsements, press features, events, book tour, or anything else! I still pinch myself every now and then just to know if this is actually my life. It's all because of you.

Garima Bhatt, my digital media marketer, and Almira Ebio Manduriao, Head of Sales, thank you for working on bringing my book to readers with your expertise!

Manasi Mathur, who designed the cover of my book, thank you for the beautiful cover you made. You didn't just do the story justice, but somehow captured the very essence of it. Thank you. (Plus, yellow is my fave color!)

Swadha Singh, Ishani Bhattacharya, Divya Gaur, and the others whose names I may never know who made this dream come true for me, thank you for all the hard work you've put into this book. What people don't know about publishing a book is that so much work goes on in the background—layout, copyediting, proofreading, checking signature proofs, the administrative, legal, and accounting work, etc.—and a lot of it is pushed to the background in favor of the shinier parts of book publishing. I appreciate everything that you do for my book. Without you, we wouldn't be here. Without you, there would be no publishing industry. Thank you so very much.

Jen Chan, Nicee, and Ela Bianca, you read my story when it was in its earliest, most shameful drafts all the way to the very end. Your insights and inputs are really what made this story what it is today. This book wouldn't exist if you hadn't helped with it.

Mom, Dad, Jem, Jas, Lolamommy, Tita Jane, and my entire family, thank you for tolerating me when I'm on my writing sprints. Know that that this is not going to stop anytime soon.

Mina Esguerra and the entire Romance Class community, the community came just in time when I was feeling so low and jaded by the writing process. Romance Class reminded me of why I wanted to write stories in the first place. This community is so supportive and loving. It feels so much like a family. I'm glad I was a part of it, even if it was just for a little bit.

Koko and Ian, June, James, Lio, Gem, Marc, Bea, Ms. Dina, Ms. Lotte, Ms. Rose, Ms. Jen, thank you for believing that I could actually do this—write a book and publish it. We've made so many books together in the past nine years, and it's still so surreal that I have my own.

Mrs. Emerita Tagal, my favorite high school English teacher who tolerated my twenty-page essays for homework, I wouldn't have become a writer if you didn't believe I could. It started with you. Look at where we are now!

Lynn Painter, I can't believe I'm writing your name here. Pinch me—no, slap me! I must be dreaming. Thank you so much for your constant support and endorsement of my story. It means so, so, so much.

Mickey Ingles, Catherine Dellosa, and Mae Coyuito, thank you for your support of this super noob author. I barely know what I'm doing, but you have been so supportive and helpful in this process. Thank you so much!!!

The romance community is so supportive and as a debut author, I count my lucky stars to have such fantastic authors helping me and my book. Samantha Young, M.A. Wardell, Ivy Ngeow, Durjoy Datta, Jenn McKinlay, Nicolas DiDomizio, thank you for being so generous with your time, energy and effort to support a nobody author from this tiny, tiny country on the other side of the world. I felt like I was dreaming when I was typing all your names here. How is this possible?

Ali Hazelwood and Tessa Bailey, never in my wildest dreams would I ever imagine seeing your names on my Instagram feed—let alone imagine you leaving comments, sharing my posts, and even following my small account! What is happening right now? Whatever it is, I am so grateful for it!

The entire book community—Bookstragrammers and Booktokers and book bloggers and bookworms everywhere—who have been so generous with their reviews and creative posts and reels, thank you for liking, sharing, commenting, and everything else that you do.

And you, dear reader. Maybe it was destiny that we met through this book, maybe it's just our mutual love for love stories and second chances and romance that got us here. Whatever it is, I'm so glad we've met.